The House of Gre
Written By B.Gre

This is a work of fiction. Similarities to real people, places, or events are entirely coincidental.

THE HOUSE OF GRENVILLE

First edition. April 19, 2024.

Copyright © 2024 B. Green.

ISBN: 979-8224905522

Written by B. Green.

Table of Contents

The House Of Grenville (Silk and Silver, #1) 1
Chapter 1: 2
Chapter 2: 6
Chapter 3: 13
Chapter 4: 22
Chapter 5: 27
Chapter 6: 33
Chapter 7: 43
Chapter 8: 51
Chapter 9: 57
Chapter 10: 61
Chapter 11: 65
Chapter 12: 73
Chapter 13: 77
Chapter 14 81
Chapter 15: 85
Chapter 16: 89
Chapter 17: 96
Chapter 18: 102
Chapter 19: 105
Chapter 20: 109
Chapter 21: 113
Chapter 22: 117
Chapter 23: 123
Chapter 24: 127
Chapter 25: 135
Chapter 26: 138
Chapter 27: 141
Chapter 28: 146
Chapter 29: 161
Chapter 30: 167

Chapter 31: 174
Chapter 31: 181
Chapter 33: 189

This Book is dedicated to all the women out there, breaking free of their own generational curses.

This book contains the following trigger warnings;

- Attempted Rape
- Murder
- Gore
- Explicit Sex
- Toxic Relationship
- British Humour

Chapter 1:

The sound of rusted metal on metal is enough to chill the bones of even the coldest of mass murderers. Yet I remember how my Dad didn't even flinch when he was brought here to Durham Prison on my 16th birthday. My feet drag as I walk behind the other convicts' friends and family. I don't want to be here, but I have to say goodbye because today's the day I leave Birmingham and the Garrick name behind. *Let's get this shit show over with.*

Mum had refused to come in with me, she said that she couldn't face more than one farewell today. Her delicate disposition has only worsened over time in my Dad's absence. Four years later she's a shell of the woman she used to be, all the fire and light you'd expect a drug lord's wife to have was taken away in the back of the riot van with him.

As I tap my foot in the queue, I try not to think about the life sentence he gets to spend in this soul sucking place.

"Ah, Louisa Garrick, great to see you again. Is today the day?" The cheerful voice of Faridah, the prison guard still on my Dad's payroll- calls from behind the bulletproof glass to signal that it's my turn.

She waves me forward while writing my information on the visitors form. I smile awkwardly as I approach, ignoring the mutters from the other disgruntled visitors.

"Your Dad's in the usual room, head straight in." Being a Garrick has its perks: no stop and search, a private visiting room, no guards hovering around us. At least what little money my brother Frankie is making now is keeping Dad safe. It makes the guilt a little easier to swallow knowing that he has protection in the roughest prison in Britain.

I head to the side door and push it open, my Dad's body engulfs me in an embrace before I've crossed the threshold.

"Hello, princess." Dad kisses my cheek and hugs me tighter. I bury my face in him, drinking in that familiar comforting scent of his. I wonder when we'll get this opportunity again.

"Hiya Dad, I brought your snacks!" I say, trying to sound upbeat, but he pulls a face that tells me he sees right through me. He grips each side of my face and looks me up and down with nothing but admiration in his eyes.

"So, off to the big fancy place today then. I couldn't be more proud, you know. The first girl in our family to be educated and not just educated- going to the best school money can buy!" He rubs his hands together, the gold sovereigns on his fingers clinking as he sits down at the table in the middle of the room.

I smirk a little at my achievement as I put my backpack down on the table and pull out his favourite flavour pot noodles and spicy crisps.

"Ooo good haul this time, girl. I had that last guard sacked for refusing to let you in with the goods, the fucking prick. Can't a man just enjoy his daughter bringing in his favourite snacks?" he chuckles as if the man's job meant nothing to the family he probably has. I watch him rifle through the bag, pulling out his favourite packet of cigarettes.

"Oh you know how to treat your old Dad, don't you?" He grins.

"Don't tell mum, she'll kill me if she finds out I'm not helping you quit. I just wanted to make sure you're fully stocked for a while, I'm not sure when I'll get a chance to visit with all my studies."

He pauses and looks up at me, his face suddenly serious and deadly. "I don't want you back here unless it's because you've found a loophole in the bail conditions. You need to focus on this, Louisa, your brother's great but he's losing his grip on Birmingham, he's too hot headed. I need to be out of here to protect him before he lands himself in the shit." I nod.

"I know what I have to do," I say a little too bluntly, the weight of my family's legacy resting on my shoulders. A legacy I want nothing to do with, but I owe him this. Guilt crashes down on me like an anvil.

The door opens and a guard comes in, he doesn't look at me, no doubt an order he was given. "Sir, Malachi has stepped out of line again. How would you like us to proceed?" The guard stands to attention like the well seasoned soldier he is.

The name Malachi rings a bell, but there's been so many new gangs popping up it's hard to keep track. Maybe he's one of *his* men. I wouldn't rule that out, his grasp on Birmingham's underbelly has grown dramatically since Dad's sentence. He even has Frankie working for him now. If only I'd paid more attention to Frankie's ramblings about stabbings and raids at the dinner table, his way of "working" is chaotic compared to my Dad's. Frankie is more of a "punch now, think later" kind of guy, whereas Dad was cool and calculated when it came to unpredictable situations- like keeping his soldiers in line. Most of them abandoned us after he got sent down, leaving us to fend for ourselves against the vultures that tried to get their hands on the top spot.

To his credit, Frankie has done his best to hold it down until we can find a loophole and get Dad out, but my research can only take me so far. I've failed miserably to even get him granted a lower sentence. When they threatened my life, Frankie didn't hesitate. He stepped down from the top without blinking, but now I owe it to him to help him out of the trouble he so often finds himself. Another reason to knuckle down into the books, not that I mind. Books are my sanctuary. I get to live a thousand lives far away from Birmingham and the burdens that come with being a Garrick.

My dad pinches the bridge of his nose and sighs. "Fuck sake! Can I not have half an hour with my daughter without you lot interrupting?

Bunch of silly cunts, the lot of you, not got two brain cells to put together!" he shouts and I watch the man flinch. Dad gets to his feet and rolls up the sleeves of his orange jumpsuit. "Sorry, Angel, I've got to go sort this before this place crumbles down." He walks round and kisses me on the cheek again. "I'm proud of you for stepping up for the family. It doesn't go unnoticed. Keep your head down there and remember, you're a fucking Garrick, you don't answer to anyone, do you understand?"

He rests his forehead against mine and I feel tears threatening to fall, not out of sadness, out of rage. I only have myself to blame for this mess. I've dedicated the last four years of my life to getting my Dad out of here and that dedication will only end when he is dead.

Chapter 2:

The wrought iron gates of hell were the only thing standing between our very old, dusty Ford focus and the home to the elite-Grenville University. I draw squiggly lines into the condensation of the car window to distract myself as they open in front of us.

"Are you nervous, Lou?" my Mum asks, taking her eyes off the winding road for a second to glance my way.

"No, I'll be fine once I find my room." I keep my answer short, my eyes fixed on the huge gothic building coming into view.

There's no denying that this place is impressive, the pictures online not doing it any justice. A gasp escapes my lips as I take it all in. My stomach flips as I realise I'm probably going to get lost once I'm inside. I can't think of anything more anxiety inducing than being late for a lecture, especially on the first day.

Shaking the thought away, I remind myself of the floor plans that I had spent weeks religiously studying since receiving my acceptance letter. "I'm going to miss you, you know." I give my Mum a big smile, wondering when I'd hear her thick Birmingham accent again.

As we begin the drive up to the carpark, I do my best to avoid stares from the other students meandering around. They don't even try to hide their disapproval as our exhaust leaves a trail of thick, black smoke behind us. Yes, we probably have the most non-eco friendly car known to man, and as we park between a Mercedes and a Rolls Royce, my cheeks heat as I realise just how noisy the car is. Any chance of blending in is now out of the question.

Mum gives me a knowing smile as the engine cuts off and drops her eyes to her lap, she clearly feels the stares too. "Do you want me to come in with you?" she asks, a silent plea in her eyes to say no. My Mum is by far the most self-conscious person I know, as much as I'd love for her to come in and hold my hand the entire time, I think she'd cry if she was so much as looked at the wrong way.

I place a hand on her shoulder, a silent understanding between the two of us as I give her a reassuring smile. "It's fine. I know where I'm going, you have a long journey back anyway," I say quietly, trying my best to hold in my need for nurturing.

She places her soft hand on my cheek and her eyes well up, I smile back, but refuse to cry. "If it's too much, you ring me and I'll come and get you. Remember what Frankie said, Lou, there's always a job there for you if this doesn't work out."

Money laundering and drug dealing? Great. I know she's trying to be reassuring, but I can't think of anything worse than working for my older brother. He's one of the many reasons I decided to leave Birmingham and applied for this scholarship in the first place. There is only one way for us to leave the messy back streets of my home town, and that's with my brain.

"I'll call him if I need him," I lie as I bring Mum in for a squeeze. Daydreams of Frankie showing up here with his crew flash behind my closed eyes, the tracksuits alone would be enough for anyone to stop and stare around here.

"Remember who you are, I'd hate for you to lose yourself to these posh twats."

I huff a laugh, burying my face in her long brown hair, memorising the smell of her sweet apple perfume. I finally peel myself off her, but keep my eyes down. My throat tightens as I push back my own stupid tears. I'm well aware I'm on my way into the snake pit and that I can't show any weaknesses here. "I'll see you soon," I say as I grab the heavy backpack that's filled with my favourite annotated books. I see Mum nod out the corner of my eye and hear the sounds of her quiet sniffs as I get out of the car.

I walk to the back and pop open the boot, pulling out my little life that's been squeezed into one suitcase. I don't look back as I begin my walk through the sea of students towards the entrance.

As I stare up at the imposing towers, my brain giddy as facts about mediaeval architecture rush through at a thousand miles per second. A part of me is still in disbelief that something this beautiful can exist in a world like ours, let alone that I get to call this place home for the next three years.

I ignore the loud rumble of the engine starting up again, as well as the low steady beat of my Mum's 70s music as I finally walk up the steps into the building. What little confidence I had left is soon non-existent as I suddenly become all too aware of my ripped jeans and plain grey t-shirt. Looking around at everyone, I clearly didn't get the dress code memo. Every single person here is dressed like they're going to the races. Most women sport classy, figure-hugging, but modest, dresses. I can only spot one girl wearing trousers, but even they look like they cost twice the amount of our rent a month, if not more. Yes, it's so clear I'm the token poor girl here.

Instead of feeding my insecurities, I turn my attention back to the building, it is, after all, the oldest university in Britain. My gaze follows the beautiful arches that frame the perpendicular style ceiling all the way to the stained glass windows, depicting various saints I can't wait to study more on. An exuberant staircase sits in the middle of the room, the carved wooden figures that are etched into the bannister looking like the kind you get on the front of pirate ships.

"Do you think those candles are paraben free?"

The light airy voice from behind me startles me, I turn to see a very thin, very blonde, very beautiful, tall woman who looks like she's straight out of the pages of a fashion magazine. I glance up at her, feeling smaller than 5'3" and regret wearing my old, comfy trainers as she towers over me. I can't put my finger on her expression, it looks... friendly? "Are you talking to me?" I ask, just to clarify so I don't make an idiot out of myself.

"Yes. Do you think the candles are paraben free? I've heard they're toxic to the environment." She smiles, okay yes, friendly.

I glance over at the highly polished candelabra sitting on a table next to a large bouquet of lilies. One of the facts I memorised from the Grenville University brochure comes out like word vomit. "Yes they are, they're made from coconut soy wax, the only biodegradable candle wax on the market."

She cocks an eyebrow. "How do you know that?" she asks.

"Oh, um, I read about it in the leaflet they sent out." I swallow, wondering if I said the wrong thing.

"That's an odd little fact to remember." Her eyes roam to take in the rest of me, it's not silent judgement she gives off, it seems more like curiosity.

"I have a good memory," I say flatly.

Luckily, she smiles again and holds out her hand for me to shake. "I'm Corinthia Stanley," she says, still beaming as I shake her hand a little too eagerly.

"I'm Louisa," I respond, praying my palms aren't sweaty.

"As in Louisa Garrick?".

How does she know who I am?

"Yes," I say tentatively.

"You're my roommate for the next year! I got my allocation a little early." She waves a slip of paper she's holding in the air.

"Oh! That's great! I haven't gotten mine yet, I was wondering where I'd be put." I smile back, praying she isn't one of those mean girls that pretends to be your friend.

The noise in the entrance grows louder by the second, as more students begin to arrive, the atmosphere turning electric. Then it stops, it's abrupt, making me wonder if I've suddenly gone deaf. I chance a glance at Corinthia, hoping she knows what's going on, but her gaze is fixed at the top of the staircase. As I follow where she's looking, I hear a gentle clicking of high heels. When the source comes into view, I regret my outfit even more. It's Professor Daphne, in the flesh. The highest paid professor in the university, the one with all the balls. I can't get over how much the pictures in the leaflet had done her an absolute injustice, she looks much younger than her headshot. Her ebony hair is styled the same, slicked back meticulously into a neat low bun at the back, the classy emerald green dress she wears complimenting her dark skin beautifully. This woman radiates power, and she shows that in every single step she takes.

She raises an eyebrow as she scans the crowd, coming to rest three steps from the bottom so she stands at least a foot higher than the rest of us, maybe more like two or three for me. My heart skips a beat as her gaze snags mine and it feels like she's staring into my soul. We hold eye contact for only a moment before she continues.

The room seems to hold its breath, waiting for her to speak.

"Welcome, students, to Grenville University," Professor Daphne starts, pausing for a moment as the crowd starts clapping. I think I hear a whistle or two accompanying it too.

"You should be proud of yourselves, you were each handpicked by our professors out of millions of applications. You are here because you are the best of the best. Among you stand the next great leaders of our country. The next ones to set foot on new planets, to find cures for deadly diseases." A low murmur of agreement echoes throughout the students. "But... it will come at a price." The room stills again at her change of tone. So quiet, I can hear my own heart pounding in my ears. "Grenville will help mould you into your deepest desires, but first you will be broken. Tested. Pushed to your absolute limits. Everything you think you know about the world will change." I shuffle on the spot uncomfortably as her eyes meet mine again as she speaks that last sentence, but I force myself not to break the contact. "Now, we've done things a little differently this year, as usual you've all been sorted into various Wings in the university, based entirely on your academic achievements and personality."

Personality? I don't remember filling out a personality page on the application... I'd definitely remember that. Plus, if they've already put me with Corinthia, the most beautiful girl here, who the fuck do they think I am?

"We also opened our applications to the masses this year, allowing one student to join us from an underprivileged background with the scholarship of their dreams."

Oh god, no. No, no, no.

"Louisa, can you come up here please?"

My stomach drops as she smiles at me, beckoning me to join her. The feel of a thousand eyes on me burns holes in my body, as I make my feet move towards her.

I stand on the step below her, my cheeks thoroughly red and sweat forming on my brow as I turn back to the crowd and look out. I choose to focus my attention on the closed doors, lifting my chin slightly, showing no weakness. I can show no weakness.

"This is Louisa Garrick, she's our-" Professor Daphne is cut off as the doors to the entrance fly open dramatically. Then in he walks... tall, imposing, beautiful. Like an Angel of Death sweeping into the entrance hall, dressed in an all black suit and long black trench coat. His silver eyes search through the crowd and his nostrils flare as they meet mine for a split second. The crowd parts and for a moment it's like he's walking towards me, only me. Like we are the only two people in the room. He stops a few steps down and Professor Daphne utters a sigh of disapproval from beside me.

"Mr Grenville, so nice of you to finally join us."

His eyes are on her then, hard and unrelenting as he tilts his head back slightly. "Some of us have more important things to attend to," he sighs and flicks a spec of invisible dust from his coat.

He sounds bored, how can anyone be bored of this?! Wait... did she just say Grenville? As in the university? Holy shit... He snaps his gaze back to me then, tilting his head ever so slightly. His eyes rake over me, and I feel so exposed despite being fully clothed. My skin feels like it's on fire. When he looks in my eyes again, I shiver under the coldness of it.

"Let's get one thing straight Mr Grenville, just because your name is on this building does not mean you will be treated any differently from the other students here. I believe you're in Silver Wing, correct?" she asks, her tone clipped.

"Yes, what other wing would I be in?" a tiny gasp ripples through the other students, while Grenville glares at Professor Daphne.

God is he always this arrogant? Why is he acting like he isn't speaking to an award winning philanthropist? Pig.

"Your wing will be punished accordingly for your tardiness." His only response is a smirk as he rolls his tongue across the inside of his cheek. The room has stood to attention, so silent you could hear a pin drop.

"As I was saying, Louisa Garrick is our Scholarship student this year. Although her background is... unique... her mind is as sharp, if not sharper than, all of you put together."

I blush and look at my feet.

"There will be a feast this evening, in honour of this historic moment."

A feast? The blood continues to rush to my face and she continues.

"I expect you all to attend. Louisa, join me in my office in an hour will you? Corinthia will show you the way."

A nervous flutter begins in my stomach.

. "Of course, may I step down now?" I ask tentatively.

She raises an eyebrow and nods. I take my place back at Corinthia's side, noticing a scoff from the front of the crowd. I don't need to turn around to know who it's from.

Chapter 3:

The walk to our room in Emerald Wing seems to take forever. Corinthia takes her time showing me the building along the way, pointing out the library and separate study rooms dotted around- I didn't have the heart to tell her that I already had this place memorised from the moment I'd gotten my acceptance letter.

When we finally reach our room, I roll my neck and shoulders praying there is a decent shower in here. But all thoughts of that plan empty from my head because this is unlike any other dormitory I've ever seen. My mouth hangs open at the size of it.

We walk straight into a living room decorated with two plush navy blue chesterfields separated by a dark wooden coffee table. Despite the size, it's cosy. I guess due to the smart use of dark colours. Large bookshelves line the walls, each filled with scriptures that look older than the building. My eyes fall on the two desks facing out of the floor to ceiling windows, on one of them is a silver laptop wrapped beautifully in a red and black bow and resting beside a stack of brand new text books. I grab the scroll next to it and rip the candle wax seal open, not taking the time to appreciate the decadence of it.

"Welcome to Grenville, Miss Garrick."

Short and sweet, I guess. As I start to get the bow off, I suddenly remember that I'm not alone, hearing the gentle clinking of glasses coming from another room. I freeze on the spot and tentatively make my way into the kitchen. Beautiful dark marble countertops greet me. I try to play it cool by leaning on the kitchen island in the middle of the room, but my eyes wander up to the silver utensils hanging from above.

Mum would have a fit if she got her hands on this kitchen, baking has always been her passion and something we shared an interest in while I was growing up. We would spend hours making dad's subordinates blueberry muffins, I remember the way their eyes would close as they smelt the delicious baked goods upon arrival, she would mother them like she did us- telling them to wash the blood from their hands before they touched her hard work.

My eyes snag on the large electric mixing bowl, I don't have to go mooching in the cupboards to know they probably have everything you need to start your own cake business here.

"Here, for the nerves." Corinthia's hand is outstretched, holding the stem of a wine glass filled with a sweet smelling red liquid.

I take it from her tentatively, although she's been nice so far, I know exactly what the people here think of me. She's clearly from 'Old Money', the kind of girl that belongs to a family that has been brought up for generations thinking a very specific thing about the working class. 'Vermin sheep' I believe was the term used in a scandalous article written about our current politicians.

I take a sip of my drink and shivers run through my body as my mind wanders back to those hateful grey eyes. Assessing me. Hating me. Why should I give a shit? I deserve to be here just as much, if not more than, anyone else. I guess I kind of am from a family fuelled by generational wealth, even if that wealth was obtained illegally the difference between us couldn't be that vast? Well, I guess it is, we don't have that kind of wealth anymore.

But at least we still had my brains, the top of every single subject at secondary school and sixth form. *I deserved to be here and I will not let some pompous grey eyed prick ruin that.*

"Are you okay? You seem on edge." Corinthia's sing-song voice pulls me back down to earth. I give her a small smile. "I'm incredibly overwhelmed if I'm honest. This room is... excessive," I admit, my cheeks heating. To my surprise she places a hand on my shoulder and gives a little squeeze. I should appreciate the kind gesture but my stubbornness screams at me not to accept her pity. I shove that part of me down and accept this stranger's physical touch. I do not need to be showing off that hereditary Garrick temper on the first day...

"I know it's a lot, especially as you're... not used to this kind of thing," Corinthia says. "But I'm here to help you with that, Grenville doesn't do things in halves- it's lavish and pushes the obscenity to the limits. The kind of wealth you see here is child's play compared to what some of the families here have experienced. If you're going to survive here, you have to be smarter and harder to the world."

The fuck? Harder to the world? I'm pretty sure I've seen it all. I don't think she was scrubbing blood from her mum's kitchen floor at age 7 after one of her dad's outbursts.

"I'm sorry, I didn't mean to upset you! I'm honestly just trying to help." Her eyes are wide, seeming genuinely upset at the fact she hit a nerve with me. What is the game here?

"It's fine, like you said, I have to get used to it. I'm sure I'll have worse thrown at me over the next three years." It comes out bitchier than I mean it too so I tag a reassuring smile on the end of it. *Not everyone has an agenda, Lou.*

"Let me show you your room." Her eyes sparkle with delight as she changes the subject. She turns on her heels and heads back into the living room, going over to the oldest looking bookcase. She pops her hand on top of a book and pulls it down in a manner that's similar to those girls you see on TV game shows that show you the prize. I hear a soft thud as the door parts from the wall.

The book is a lever? How fucking cool is this?

The door swings inward to reveal a gorgeous bedroom. My bedroom apparently. It's breathtaking. The inviting four poster bed is filled with the softest and bounciest looking pillows. I don't wait to look at anything else as I run up to it and leap into the air, landing back down onto the cloud like mattress. It's like floating on air. I can't help the gleeful sigh I let out as I gaze up at the emerald green canopy above.

"You have your own bathroom just in here and your wardrobe..."

I sit up in time just as Corinthia opens up another concealed door in the room. Why are all the doors here secret? I'm not complaining, but why does it feel like this is to give us as many hiding spots as possible?

I gasp as I find the wall in the wardrobe fully stocked. Scrambling off the sheets, not giving a shit about Corinthia's little chuckle, I make my way inside to see the attire up close.

"Do they do this for all of the students?" I ask, running my hand over the expensive looking clothes hanging up on the rail.

"No, but Professor Daphne helped me arrange it all. She doesn't think it's fair that we're such an exclusive school. She thinks of you as her little experiment. If you succeed here, she can open up spots for more students next year."

They did this for me? Tears burn my eyes, both out of embarrassment and exhaustion. "Thank you, Corinthia. This is a lot to take in," I manage to say.

She cringes, "Call me Cora, please. I know this is probably hard to believe, but I want to help. I want to be your friend. The class divides in this world are too extreme, I want to be part of breaking the barriers."

Something flashes in her eyes that makes me second guess how much truth there is in that statement. I wonder what her real reasoning for doing this is? My mind reels at all of the possibilities a girl like her has at her feet.

"Shall I help you pick something out? We have to go and meet Professor Daphne before we start getting ready for the ball." Cora pulls out a pair of brown houndstooth trousers that flow out at the bottom and a tight white high neck tank top that leaves the arms bare. She lays them on the bed and assesses them with what I assume to be expert scrutiny. "Why don't you freshen up? Deciding on the shoes will take me a moment." Cora doesn't look at me, she places a hand under her chin as she stares at the outfit laid flat on the bed. "Sure, I'll err just grab my washbag." I mutter, making my way to my suitcase. "Don't bother, I had my personal assistant grab you some things from duty free on my way here." She grins. "Do you live abroad?" I ask as I back away from the bed towards the bathroom. "No, but I'm hardly in the country. I'm just back from Bali actually, have you been?" I open the large white leather wash bag on the vanity. My eyes widen at the collection inside. I make a mental note to google what the hell toner is. "No, um we used to go to benidorm, when I was little though." *Before my father was sent to prison for something he didn't do and we went completely broke.*

I close the bathroom door and try to push away the feeling that there's something seriously wrong here. The laptop, the clothes, the secret doors... there has to be an ulterior motive here because I know these people don't accept just anyone into their inner circles.

I begin scrubbing my face with scented cleanser from the bag labelled "24 carat gold Cleanser."

Why would someone like Cora want to help me? Wouldn't it be more fun if she just sat back and watched me fail at attempting to fit in with the elite?

I have to be smart about it if I'm going to dig deeper. I need to let them think they've bought my friendship, my obedience.

※

I FIDGET UNCOMFORTABLY in the red and black high back chair in Professor Daphne's office, the clothes cling to my body in ways that I had never imagined possible. The material felt nice but that's about as far as it went. Maybe I only felt like this because it wasn't my usual jeans and T-shirt look.

Professor Daphne's words from earlier hang over me, the ones about being broken before we can be the best. I have no doubt the clothing situation was just the beginning... I listen to the ticking sound of the small silver clock on top of the black filing cabinet in the corner. My palms are clammy in anticipation as she finally enters the room, almost late.

She takes her seat behind the imposing desk, assessing me with what seems to be curiosity- as long as it's not hatred, I'll go with it. Nobody can deny she's an intimidating woman. Her qualifications alone are impressive, as well as being utterly gorgeous like the rest of the women here.

I fold my hands in my lap, praying for her to cut the awkward silence.

"Is your room to your liking?" she finally asks. "I wanted to give you the full Grenville experience but other members of the faculty thought it would be inappropriate to put you in the Silver Wing, Emerald Wing was our compromise."

She doesn't lean back in her chair, there's nothing casual about this woman at all. I unconsciously shift in my seat, adjusting my posture to mimic hers. Psychology 101 right?

"It's a beautiful room and thank you for the laptop and clothes, it was really unnecessary..."

She holds a hand up, cutting me off. My mouth goes dry and I swallow hard. "Rule number one, never shy away from gifts."

I flinch a little at the sudden harshness of her tone. "I'm sorry... I-" Why am I stuttering like a fool, she closes her eyes, curls her lip and holds up her hand to stop me again. I clamp my mouth shut, waiting for her to speak.

"Rule number two, never apologise for anything. You're a Grenville girl now, Grenville girls don't apologise."

I sigh in frustration at the sudden list of rules being shoved in my face.

"Is there a problem, Louisa?" I swallow the Birmingham attitude, as much as I want to call her a bitch and leave the room, I won't give her the satisfaction. I think about my response carefully.

"I'm not sure I understand what's going on here, Professor." I try to keep my tone light and airy, but of course I fail miserably. Professor Daphne rises from her seat and begins to wander over to her framed achievements that adorn the walls, every step purposeful and elegant.

"Do you understand why you're here, Louisa?" She keeps her back to me, allowing a small reprieve from her intimidating gaze.

"Well, my grades are impeccable. My application, impressive. I have extensive work experience and numerous extracurricular achievements..." but that damn perfectly polished hand rises up to stop me, AGAIN. I snap my mouth shut *again* and feel my teeth grinding together to keep it all in.

"Your naivety is endearing, but it will get tiresome after a while. I suggest finding a new personality trait if you are wanting to survive here." *This fucking bitch!* "You are not here because you were the smartest applicant. Despite what the reports of this prestigious university say to the tabloids, you do not have to be smart to succeed. Quite the opposite actually. Everyone knows you only need a good name, and all the doors in the world open for you." Her expression is hard and unrelenting. "You were chosen because you fit the profile that the board wanted, they want somebody who they can mould into the ultimate Grenville girl. Someone who will do anything to get their father out of prison."

Professor Daphne pulls a thick looking file from the draw beneath her desk and slams it down on top of the hardwood. I flinch at the noise. *Shit, there goes my anonymity here.*

"The board wants someone they think they can manipulate, the old men that sit at the head of the table grow tired of the leaders in the world. You were chosen because you are easy to leverage."

I stare at the floor, was this some kind of sick joke? I've worked my ass off getting into this school, for what? So I could be taught to be a good little puppet, not a chance. I rise from my seat, my fathers words echoing in my head

Remember you're a fucking Garrick.

"Thank you for the opportunity, Professor Daphne. But I think I'll have to decline. I'll grab my things and leave right away." I try to keep my voice from breaking as my vision blurs. *I've failed miserably.*

"Rule number three, never run away from an opportunity to get the upper hand." She grins a cheshire cat-like smile, her pearlescent teeth gleaming like they're about to sink into my throat.

What little grip I have on my temper finally snaps.

"Is this some kind of elaborate humiliation tactic? I will not stand here and be made to feel like nothing by someone who has no idea what I've done to get out of Birmingham." My chest heaves up and down at my admission.

Professor Daphne clicks her fingers in the air.

"That's why I chose you. Because you're here with the goal to change the lives of everyone you can, and I can help you do it. You and I are on the same page, Louisa- we want the same thing. For everyone in this country to have an equal opportunity, no matter if they are descended from Gypsies or from the Royal Family."

This place is giving me whiplash... and I haven't even been here two hours. So she likes me because I'm feisty? Does she really believe I can help her change all of those things? I came here with a clear goal, perhaps it wouldn't be so bad if I let them take advantage of me. Maybe they would get dad out of prison sooner if they did.

I returned to my seat, wondering if Cora was aware of my family history. What a stupid thought, of course she fucking did. Daphne hand picked her to help me, I'm sure she wouldn't have gone into this blind. I wonder what the Professor has on her...

"While you study here you will attend lessons each week on how to become the perfect socialite. This means learning how to walk, talk, eat, dress, host. You are miles behind the other girls here, but I'm sure you're a fast learner. Corinthia will help you pick up the slack where she can. You'll check in with me here, once a week. If your extra lessons start to affect your academic lessons, tell me and I'll mark your assignments myself. Do this for the next three years, and your family will have a get out of jail free pass for the rest of their lives." She looks down at the blank piece of paper on her desk, pursing her lips as she takes a pen from her pen pot and starts writing.

Am I dismissed?

"Why the extra lessons?" I blurt before I can stop them, my accent coming on thick. "Why would you help me with that? To fit in here, I mean."

She doesn't look up when she says "Let's just say, I need someone on my side on the inside. I can't let my protégés into high society without knowing how to pour a cup of tea, can I? My terms are simple, Louisa. Do the lessons, excel at them, blend in and in three years time your family is safe to return to pushing powder and pills." She waves a hand without awaiting my response to her ridiculous terms. I guess I didn't have a choice but to accept them.

I say nothing as I leave the room, my cheeks no doubt flushed pink with the encounter. Cora is waiting outside for me, perched on the edge of her seat, ankles folded behind her, perfectly accentuating the length of her legs.

"Was it that bad?" she asks.

"Yes." I mutter as I stomp off back towards my room, wanting nothing more than to stop my mind's reeling with a hot shower.

Chapter 4:

Apparently scrubbing my skin red raw in the shower isn't enough to stop my overactive brain. In fact, the bathroom has made me more agitated. The obscenity of this place was starting to get on my tits. I've no doubt each tile in this room was probably hand carved by some elite overpriced Italian man that charged £100 an hour and £1000 per tile or something stupid like that. I feel bitter about my first day, being assigned a "buddy" who I don't know if I can truly trust. Being told I'm just here to be Professor Daphne's puppet. What use can she possibly have for me? I have more questions than answers at this point, and the way I see it is I have two options.

Option 1- Call Frankie to pick me up and quit this whole ridiculous thing and deal with the comments back home about how I couldn't hack it.

Option Two- play them at their own game, make them think I've taken them up on their stupid offer meanwhile bring them all down from the inside. While option two is definitely preferable, I have no idea where the fuck I'd start. Or who I'm trying to take down... I know nobody at the top, I doubt the person running the show is Professor Daphne which only raises more questions.

Before I can make my choice, a knock on my bedroom door makes it for me. Cora comes bursting in with another girl, neither of them giving a shit that I'm standing in a towel.

"Lou, this is Belladonna Yen." She lets out a little squeal and claps her hands like a seal.

Brows knitting together, I clutch my towel as I look at Belladonna fucking Yen. Of course she's here. Belladonna is the heiress to her aunt's hotel chain fortune, quite possibly the richest woman in the country. Her dark eyes gleam as she takes me in.

I hold my chin high, refusing to let this bitch make me feel self conscious.

"Well, she's not a total loss, Cora. There's plenty to work with here." She saunters into the room, her ridiculously long dark hair blowing unnaturally as she starts to circle me as if she's a lion and I a deer. Her dark skin looks like silk, nott a blemish in sight. "I hear you're the one who's going to bring down the patriarchy." She runs her tongue over her teeth, as she continues looking me up and down.

I glance at Cora, wondering if this is supposed to be a secret.

"Don't worry, this affects Bella as well. She's here to help with... this..." she explains, waving her hands in front of me.

"I don't need any extra help, besides, I haven't agreed to anything yet." I raise my best haughty eyebrow at them both as they share a look.

Bella let out a laugh, just as poisonous as her name suggests.

"Oh she's feisty, I like this one." Cora beams at her.

"Told you she'd be great, just needs a little preening." I clench my fists as my breath quickens, I think I've had enough of people chatting shit about my appearance today. "SHE is standing right here, I'm not a bush in need of trimming you arseholes."

"Oh what an adorable accent, are you from the north?" Bella asks.

Letting out a frustrated "ugh" noise, I stomp away towards the closet. I yank open some drawers in search of underwear, only to find the entire drawer is full of lacy strings. How can that be comfortable?! Closing my eyes, I try to calm my rising frustration.

"Do you need some help?" Cora asks tentatively, at least she has enough respect to be wary of my mood.

"Why does she want me to do this? Why do I have to learn all of these stupid etiquette things and wear knickers that leave very little to the imagination?!" it comes out like word vomit, I don't even try to keep my accent in check.

"It doesn't make any sense," I say to nobody particular, as I grip the towel wrapped around me like it's a life jacket.

Bella sighs before saying, "Just tell her, Cora." as plonks herself and her very expensive bag down on my bed. Cora shoots her a wary look, like if she divulges the truth something awful will happen to her. I can almost see her internal battle happening.

"Fine. Come sit down," she mutters, and I follow her out of the wardrobe.

"So she can follow instructions without having a toddler tantrum?"

Rolling my eyes, I sit in the deep red chair next to the window, overlooking a large pond that I hadn't noticed earlier.

"If I'm honest Louisa, I don't know. All I know is what I've been told, which is the same as you. I was told I'd get an automatic pass on everything if I helped you."

She doesn't meet my eyes, a clear sign she's lying. But then again maybe she'd be in some sort of danger if she were to tell me how deep this shit truly goes. I'll have to earn her trust, which can only be done with time. *Looks like I'm stuck here, surrounded by a bunch of very good looking liars.*

"Daphne is trying to change the way the world works for women. She's trying to prove that if girls got the same guidance as boys they'd be able to do the same job- if not better because we can multitask..."

Bella huffs out a laugh at her friend's choice of words.

"Do you know I can't inherit my father's fortune unless I marry?"

I glance at Bella, not attempting to hide my shock as she gazes down at the floor, her mouth shut in a tight line.

"That's.. that's not right, I'm sorry." I'm genuine in my sympathy, what a shitty situation to be in.

"But you can help change that," Bella says. "You've got the brains and with our help you'll have them all eating out of your hands in no

THE HOUSE OF GRENVILLE

time so that one day! Maybe Daphne wants you to become the next Prime Minister!"

So this is political? Of course it is. *Looks like I'm every puppeteer's favourite today.*

"I'll do it," I mutter, pretending to be dense. I can dig deeper into this once I've earned their trust. Daphne never mentioned anything to do with Feminism in the meeting, she's clearly spun a web of lies to Cora to get her on board. More than likely leveraging her distaste of the marriage contract to get her to help me. But which one of Daphne's statements were true?

Bella leaps up and claps, Cora looks like she's about to pass out from the relief. *Interesting.*

"Now can someone please direct me to the drawer that houses comfortable underwear?" They both share a look and laugh, I'll admit it's a little infectious. Perhaps it wouldn't be so bad to be their friend after all.

"We're going to need Champagne for this." Bella kicks her heels off and runs to the kitchen, returning swiftly with her hands full. "Cora, fetch the Calvin Kleins, we'll break her in gently."

Before I can take a breath, a whole army of hair and make-up people usher into our living room. I'm talking two or three people for each of us. Hollywood style chairs get pulled out of nowhere. I sit at the portable dressing table the makeup artist has brought in, keeping my mouth shut as she begins to dry my hair. I hated my hair growing up, it had darkened down to a harsh ebony colour from mousy brown when I was around 7 years old, making me look like some sickly version of Snow White. Of course this was a running joke in school.

When the makeup artist starts moving towards me with sharp looking tweezers, I draw the line. "Um, absolutely not!" I say, shrinking back in my chair.

I'm relieved when Cora turns to me and says, "If you're not comfortable, it's fine."

My relief bubble is soon burst by Bella muttering, "You have to get rid of those ridiculous slugs. You can either let Francesca here do it professionally or I'll creep into your bedroom tonight and shave them off completely."

My eyes widen in horror whilst everyone else stifles a laugh and I don't doubt for a second that she wouldn't do it. Francesca shrugs and raises an eyebrow at me, I guess a little pain can't hurt? I close my eyes and nod. If this is going to work and I'm going to get to the bottom of this, I have to be all in.

"Wait!" shouts Cora, startling everyone in the room. "Francesca, get the hot wax we need to do the top lip too."

I almost shriek in horror at the gleam in Francesca's eyes as she scuttles off to some other portable station they'd set up.

I have to be all in. I chant in my head as I wait for the torture to begin.

Chapter 5:

Bella and Cora flank either side of me, my arms looped with theirs to keep my balance in the painfully high stilettos. The girls walk like they're on a catwalk, Bella doesn't show that she's already half pissed. I can't help but feel a little jealous during my Cinderella moment at how easy they both make this look. I have about as much grace and decorum as bambi on ice and boy did I feel it next to these two.

When I'd looked at myself in the mirror after the make-over session I hardly recognised myself. I felt beautiful, but extremely self conscious. The only time I had worn anything like this was at my teenage prom, I was all gangly limbs and no tits, the entire thing was one big awkward-fest.

Cora chose to wear her hair down and straight, the golden strands complimenting the baby powder blue silk gown that hugs her figure perfectly. A sexy yet sophisticated look, Bella had said. Bella has gone with a deep red ball gown that screamed "Queen of the Vampires." The corset style top cinched her tiny waist within an inch of her life. I still don't understand how she's breathing. She's swapped her long sleek black hair for a glamorous short, icy blonde pixie style cut for the occasion. It accentuates her high cheek bones phenomenally.

I didn't have a choice in how I looked tonight, every styling decision had to be Bella and Cora approved, so I was told. I'd been transfixed by Michelle, the hairdresser, as she curled, twisted and pinned my dark hair up into a fancy up-do. My dress is a midnight blue number, the bodice had off the shoulder sleeves which gave me serious fairy-tale princess vibes. That part wasn't so bad but the meringue style skirt was a little over the top for me.

Butterflies start up in my stomach as we near the tall wooden doors, I try my hardest to recite the very very quick formal dance the girls had tried to show me. I pray that I don't baulk when the music starts. As the doors open, I stare around in awe at the beautiful room. At the top, just below the stained glass windows, sits a long table that I guess is for the faculty. In the middle, there are round tables each adorned with a tall bouquet of flowers in the various colours of the different wings.

I grip the girl's arms a little tighter as I take a deep breath. They lead me over to the table with the Emerald Green roses. God, everything here is so extra! I cannot even imagine how long it took someone to get these tablecloths so crisp, do they reuse them each time or just buy new ones?

"Stop gawking like a fish and sit the fuck down," Bella whispers to me in a sing-song, her smile not faultering.

Shit. I've just been standing here staring at the fucking linen. I try to copy the other two as they slide gracefully into their chairs, but my chair makes an awful scraping noise as I pull it out. I wrinkle my nose and mutter "Sorry!" to everyone around me.

Once I've sat down, Cora, who's sitting across from me, gestures discreetly for me to remove the napkin shaped like a... peacock? Off of my plate. I try to be as delicate as I can as I fumble with it, unfolding it gently as if it's made of glass. A low cough from beside me grabs my attention.

"You don't unfold it, just give it a shake. Watch me." The Greek God-like man with the deep voice sitting next to me says, as shakes his napkin out in one fluid movement and places it down on his lap. I give him a sheepish grin as I try to do the same but to my absolute horror the damn peacock stays perfectly in place. Has someone glued this together? The man grabs my wrist gently and brings my arm over towards him and flicks out. The napkin of course unfolds and I blush from the embarrassment. *Sure I can remember every detail of the battle of Hastings, but can't shake out a napkin? Jesus, this is going to be a long night.*

"I was warming it up for you." I say, trying to brush off the hideous encounter. His dark brown eyes finally look away from me as he smiles.

"What an interesting accent, are you Irish or Cornish? I never can quite tell," he asks.

The blood drained from my face, I had forgotten to keep the accent in check again.

"Neither, I'm from Birmingham," I mutter, trying to sound a little posher than I am. What a disaster. I nervously glance up at Cora for help but she's deep in conversation with a large Rugby player looking guy next to her and I'll be damned if I take another condescending insult from Bella. As if sensing my plea for help, he thankfully breaks the awkward silence.

"I'm Sebastian Goddworthy," Sebastian takes my hand in his and plants a small kiss on the back of it. What the fuck do I do now?

"Sebby, this is Louisa," Bella introduces from next to me, her hand gently resting on my knee. "She's Cora's roommate this year."

I wince as Bella's sharp talons dig into my leg fiercely, telling me all I need to know about how this interaction is going...

"My my, Louisa, I barely recognised you after this morning. You're in good hands with these two, you'll land a rich husband in no time." He looks me up and down like I'm a piece of meat. My skin crawls.

"So far I've found the men here dull as dishwater. I'd find more thrilling conversation with a book of nursery rhymes. I assume they have one here to keep you entertained?" I grab the glass of red wine that I'd spotted out of the corner of my eye, in the dainty lady-like way I saw Cora handle her champagne flute earlier, and take a long healthy sip.

Bella bursts into a well rehearsed laughter, squeezing my leg tighter. I throw Sebastian a sweet smile and he raises an eyebrow in approval.

"You'll do well here with that wicked tongue of yours. I do enjoy a challenge." His eyes smoulder and I gulp as I realise I may be in way over my head here.

AFTER DINNER, THE BALLROOM is transformed when we walk back in, complete with a full orchestra already playing a classical version of a pop song I vaguely recognise. Everyone takes their places immediately in the middle of the room, boys on one side, girls on the other.

I glance up to see that Sebastian is directly in front of me, his face plastered with a smug smile. Did he put himself there on purpose? There's no time to question the motivations of the stranger as the lines suddenly move in unison, my feet begging me for a reprieve against the assault of the shoes. I surprise myself as I remember the steps, although I know I'm nowhere near on par with everyone else- at least I know them. I focus on repeating the pattern in my head to take my mind off of Sebastian's hand on the small of my back.

"Absolutely fascinating," he mutters.

"What is?" I ask as he twirls me effortlessly.

"I can almost hear the wheels turning in your head. Very impressive of you to remember all the steps." He leans a little closer, invading my space a little too much.

"You're invading my dance space, I'm trying very hard here not to make a complete tit out of myself." It comes out a little harsher than I intend but he doesn't seem to take offence, his eyes are practically gleaming at my venomous tone.

He says nothing else and flings me into the arms of another. I have a moment where I'm relieved to be rid of him, but it's only fleeting as I'm now face to face with a familiar silver eyed man.

I look anywhere but at him, unable to bear the hatred exuding from him as the dance continues. His hands barely touch me, as if I'm contaminated.

"The little mouse has come out to play with the snakes I see."

Why does he despise me so much? I keep quiet, focusing on getting this dance out of the way, so I can run upstairs and probably cry. I don't need to look up at him to know he's not taking his eyes from me, and it's not in a romantic way either. It's like he's trying to burn a hole through my brain.

He leans in close, a little too close, his breath sending a shiver up my spine.

"You're going to be eaten alive here, Garrick." I finally gathered some courage and looked at him. His face up close, is to die for. It's as if the man in front of me had been carved straight from marble. Perfection, if I dare say. All thoughts of his rudeness and arrogance have emptied from my brain, I forget that I'd even taken offence to him calling me by my last name; as if I were the subordinate. Now I'm all too aware of the proximity of our body's, the heat radiating from him is an excruciating temptation. If it were anyone else, this might even be the most romantic set up in the world...

"What makes you so sure of that, exactly?" I ask, giving my head a wobble and trying my best to impersonate Bella's haughtiness. He gives me a dazzling side smirk that reveals a dimple in his cheek. He sees right through me, I know it.

"Uninvited rodents tend to create problems. Just because the board wishes to welcome someone like you doesn't mean that I will extend such hospitality." His gaze hardens as he fixes it to the back wall, giving me a nice view of his chiselled jaw line. If he wasn't being such a prick right now I'd be swooning.

"I *was* invited to be here." I spit back at him. "You would get shanked the moment you set foot in Birmingham, do you know that? I may be out of my own territory here Mr. Grenville but do not insult me when you don't know me. Underestimate me or threaten me again and I'll show you just how many problems I can create for you, should you get in the way of what I want." I cock an eyebrow at him, daring him to prove me wrong. The space between us now houses a sizzling tension. A tiny flicker of something in his expression catches me off guard, too quick for me to overanalyze.

"What is it that you want?" The question catches me off guard just as the music ends and he walks away without another word. I watch him disappear into the crowd, my head filled with a thousand questions.

Chapter 6:

The sun streams through the window in my bedroom, the warmth of it brings a smile to my face. I pull back the covers as I wince, the pounding in my head increasing, -thanks to last night's champagne- as I plot to make time today to explore the grounds of the University. Unfortunately for me, the embarrassing memories of last night swim to the surface. It had certainly been more of a minefield than I'd anticipated. The conversations flowed like a dead language; skiing in the alps, talks of buying low and selling high... Who knew these were even a thing for a bunch of 19/20 year olds to be so accustomed too? It made my head spin. One girl talked about her fathers next political manoeuvre, like he was moving house.

I listen carefully as I stretch my arms to see if Cora is up yet, but I don't hear movement behind the secret door. Today was orientation, officially the beginning of solving my problems. I had flutters of excitement mixed with a healthy dose of anxiety as I headed over to the wardrobe to find something suitable to wear.

No Jeans or T-shirts here. I mused. Another reason why my training from professor Daphne couldn't come soon enough, I had to learn how to dress myself sooner or later right? I'm also sure that if I have to attend one more fancy arse dinner with no training, Grenvilles warning about being eaten alive would be happening sooner than I'd expected.

It's only a matter of time before the sharks in this place smell blood. While I might've been able to somewhat fool Sebastian, I know that Grenville didn't buy my act at all.

My phone pings from the bedside table, an eerie sense of dread washes over me. I pray it's mum, *please be her checking in and wanting the gossip*. But as I pick it up and see the name my stomach drops. Of course it's *him*. How stupid of me to think that I could move hours away and not be hounded by Frankie on my very first day.

"I need a favour." The message reads, of course he does, what else would he possibly want. Before I can reply, telling him to kindly fuck off, the phone rings. I take in a deep breath before I answer.

"What do you want?" It comes out hoarse, my throat is dry as hell. *Champagne hangover is not the one.*

"Baby sister, that's no way to greet your knight in shining armour now is it."

It's only been a few weeks since I last spoke to him, but his accent seems thicker than before.

"Did you get my text?" straight to the point it is then.

"Yes, about thirty seconds ago. What do you want?" I can't help the sigh escaping at the end.

"There's a package arriving for you today. It won't make it past the crazy security checks your place has but I need you to get your hands on it and keep it hidden for me."

I pinch the bridge of my nose.

"Always involving me in your stupid schemes. No, I'll send it back, I'm not keeping anything for you here. They do room searches here you know!" Okay that was a lie, but today was my first day, I couldn't be seen running around hiding secret packages for Frankie. I need to make a good impression for fuck sake.

"You *will* get the package and you *will* keep it there for me until I can collect it. Or do you want me showing up to meet all your new posh friends?"

The thought of my two worlds colliding almost makes me vomit. The last thing I need is Frankie showing up here, I'm sure the people here have enough questions about me.

"How the fuck am I supposed to get this parcel? I got here yesterday. I don't even know where they put the mail," I whisper-shout back, as I hear movement in the room next to mine.

"Figure it out baby sister, both our necks are on the line here. Don't let anyone find it, do you understand?" His tone shifts and it sets me on edge, as much as I despise helping him right now, I know he'll do anything to protect me.

"Okay, I'll get it. What's in the package? Are you in trouble?" I say quietly. He sighs and I can almost see his inner battle through the phone. I know he's all that stands in the way of the Birmingham underground coming to snatch me from my duck feather bed.

"Don't open it. The less you know the better if this all goes tits up."

I close my eyes as I say, "Leave it to me, I'll figure it out."

The line cuts, *no goodbyes.*

"DID YOU BRING SOMEONE back with you last night?" Cora asks, yawning as we arrive at our first lecture after picking up my jam packed schedule from Professor Daphne's office. *No visits to the lake today.*

"No, why?".

"I could have swarm I heard you talking to someone."

Shit.

"Oh, that was just my mum, calling to get all the gossip from last night." I'm shit at lying, I can only hope she hasn't had enough caffeine to notice my tell tale signs.

"Oh, are you close?" she asks, but I lie again. I don't know her well enough to unburden my family drama onto her yet. *When is a good time to tell a stranger that you're Mafia royalty?*

"Yeah, very." My answer is clearly a little too blunt as her eyes narrow slightly.

"Do you think we'll have time to go wherever they keep the post before our politics lecture? Mums sent me a care package of all my favourite snacks." I try to ramble on enough to annoy her so she's eager to change the subject.

"No way, we don't want to risk being late to Professor Carr's lecture. That man is brutal at the best of times, don't give him a reason to hate you."

The vast, musty auditorium quickens my pulse as I marvel at the size of the lecture hall. Cora suggests a seat near the back, which I'm grateful for. The less judgy eyes on me the better. As I watched the other students file in, the sense of entitlement and privilege overwhelmed me. The outfit I'd chosen suddenly felt too exposing for a first day. A beige, calf length dress with a panel of black travelling down the front of the dress, making the gold buttons stand to attention. I had gone for flat beige pumps to match and I thought Cora was about to slap me as I slung my old backpack over my shoulder. Before she could say anything- I told her that none of the ridiculous bags in that wardrobe would fit my textbooks in, let alone a laptop.

I busy myself getting everything I need out of my backpack and placing it on the wooden bench that circles the top of the auditorium, when I feel a prickling sensation up the back of my neck. There's only one person I know that gets that kind of reaction from my body. Everyone around us falls silent, I focus my eyes on the stage dead ahead.

I can feel his death glare on me, I school my features into a look of boredom. Despite my body screaming at me to run out of the room.

"Um, Lou... why is Benjamin Grenville staring at you like he's about to break every bone in your body?" Cora whispers to me out of the side of her mouth. I don't dare to turn my head.

"I don't know, he hates me! We danced last night and... let's just say it was an experience I do not want to repeat," I mutter. Then to my utter dismay, my view of the stage is blocked by the dickhead himself. He sits right in front of me, obscuring my view completely. I clench my fists until my knuckles turn white, *why does he insist on being an arsehole?*

Cora and I exchange a glance, the inner workings of Benjamin Grenville are at the bottom of my concern list right now. Surely this guy couldn't be *this* petty? It's probably all in my head. I turn my focus to Professor Carr as he begins introducing himself- not that I can see him around the enormous man in front of me.

I keep trying to crane my neck around him but he seems to shift in his seat every time I do. I press my fingernails into the palm of my hand to stop myself ripping this guy's head off. *This is going to be a long two hours.*

The lecture starts and no amount of research could have prepared me for this level of politics. Everyone's spewing out names that I've never heard of. I've ditched the laptop in favour of a notebook at this point because I cannot type fast enough to get all this information down.

"Now, let's move onto debate preparation. Be ready to disarm your opponent with words. Physical Fighting in the house of commons means you will hand in your resignation with no arguments, unless of course you don't value your career at all. Now can I have a volunteer please?" I sink into my seat a little lower as he scans the sea of faces like his eyes are some kind of x-ray machine.

"Mr. Grenville, your silence is deafening. Why don't you come up here and show us exactly why your father is the best of the best." Murmurs of anticipation ripple through the other students as their eyes are glued to his every move as he takes his place behind the podium on the right side of the stage. He stands tall and confident. There's nothing casual about his intimidating stance, he's clearly done this before. No doubt trained since birth.

"As it's your first day, Mr. Grenville. I will allow you to choose your opponent. But next week, you will all be assigned your partners by me. Before I send you out to be in charge of the country, I have to prepare you for any possible curveball's opposing political parties might throw at you."

My stomach drops, *please don't pick me.* But my silent plea's fall on deaf ears as he calls my name through the microphone on top of the podium.

"I choose Miss Garrick as my opponent today, Professor." I swallow hard and turn in bewilderment to Cora, but she's just as dumbfounded as I am. She straightens in her seat and nods at me encouragingly.

"Just think about all those useless facts you know, that will throw him off!" She whispers as she hurries me to stand. I smooth down my dress as I do, plucking what little self confidence I have left out of me as I walk quickly down the stairs and towards the stage. I catch Professor Carr's eye as I approach the podium, he gives me a sympathetic smile as I take my place.

"Mr. Grenville. You will represent the Blues. Miss Garrick. You will represent the Greens. I trust you are both up to scratch on each party's current manifesto?"

No.

"Yes, sir." I say confidently. Grenville only answers him with a nod.

"Let's debate the rising crime rate in Britain. Begin." Professor Carr gestures to him, as he takes a seat directly in front of me. My mouth dries, the auditorium is so quiet you could hear a pin drop. I take a few shaky breaths and use the podium to keep myself upright as I begin to search through the information I have stored away in my head. I turn to face Grenville, trying to get a gauge on how he's about to approach this, to see if that picturesque statue has faltered under the pressure of a thousand eyes. He glances my way and the world dissipates as I'm lost in those hateful eyes. It was then that I knew an attack was imminent.

BY THE TIME THE HUMILIATION ends, I'm left questioning what the fuck our political system even is and mentally prepare myself for a date with Google when I get back to my room.

He'd meet every single one of my points with a coy, backhanded answer. Every time I went on offence mode he'd deflect like a pro. It was like he could read my mind. God I'd have to try and dive into some psychology books on how to read non verbal communication. The only positive that came out of the horrific ordeal, was that I knew it would be a few weeks before it happened again. Next time I would make sure I was prepared for him, or whoever else might take up the job as torturer for the day.

"That was fucking awful to watch Lou, I mean really awful. Why did he lay into you like that on your first day? Do you need me to walk you to the Post room?" Cora asks delicately as we head around the corner of the corridor.

"No it's okay, I think I can find it. Thank you though. I'll meet you in Debutant Training," I say as I give her a quick smile before I scurry off. I have exactly 15 minutes before my next lesson and I already know I should be jogging to the other side of the University if I'm going to make it.

All of my rage from the previous lesson fuels my walking speed. I'm thankful that nobody can see me gasping for breath, as I reach the door to the portal room. When I walk in, I'm greeted by a very old, very stoic woman. She's impeccably dressed like the rest of the staff and her designer half moon glasses hang on the edge of her poker straight nose. She assesses me in more ways than one as I approach the desk, one of her eyes slightly twitching as her gaze falls on my backpack.

"Um, hi. Parcel for Louisa Garrick please?"

She turns on her heel, frustratingly slow and starts running her bony fingers down the cubby holes looking for my name. I tap my foot against the stone floor, counting down the minutes I have left to dump the parcel securely back in my room and make it to my first lesson on how to be a lady. Finally, after what seems like an age, she brings it over and slams it down onto her giant desk with a heavy hand. I don't know what I was expecting but it isn't this, the package is tiny! I instantly regret telling Cora it was a care package from home because what the fuck could you fit in here.

"Thank you, have a good day," I say, still staring at the parcel.

"A girl like you should be careful around here," the old lady says.

My curiosity peaks and the old woman's tone.

"What do you mean?"

"You'll see soon," she says, before turning her back on me. This place gets stranger by the minute. With my eyes still on the package I start walking out of the postal room and back into the grand arched hallway.

Pulling out my phone, I send Frankie a text letting him know I've got it, when my head collides with a muscular body and sends me arse over tit onto the floor.

"Jesus, Garrick! Can't you watch where you're going?!" The cold voice that just berated me for two hours is all too familiar. Of course it's him, who fucking else would it be?

"Are you following me or something?" I spit out as I pick myself up and grab my bag off the floor, avoiding his stare at all costs.

"As if I'd find *something* like you interesting enough to follow."

I try not to show that his words sting, "Fuck off, *Grenville*. I've had enough of your insults for one day." My accent is out in full force now, all pretence of being lady-like out the window. This man is infuriating, I've been here for one day and he's done nothing but torment me, for what? What is this guy's issue?!

"Oooh, the little Birmingham bitch has some bite. What a shame you couldn't put that vulgar mouth of yours to better use earlier." I stand as tall as I can but barely come up to his chin. "Insult me again and you'll see just how hard I *can* bite. Or was my threat last night not enough for you? Your attitude towards women is disgusting and just because your name is on the fucking building, does not mean you can call me a bitch and get away with it!" I bare my teeth a little on that last word.

I watch his tongue run across the inside of his cheek as he slowly closes the gap between us more. I take a step back not wanting him in my personal space, but he just keeps walking until my back is pressed up against the postal room door. He braces his arms against the wall on either side of me, trapping me beneath his hard body. I swallow my fear and keep eye contact with him.

"I think you'll find that I have the utmost respect for women, some would even go so far as to call it devotion or worship."

His eyes flash down to my lips as a million thoughts race through my head making it impossible to pick just one single train of thought. I try not to focus on the one in which I fantasise of all the ways he DOES worship women. My breath catches as he licks his lips and leans in even closer, is he about to kiss me? What the fuck is happening? Grenville cocks an eyebrow and gives me a devilish smirk that would rival my brothers.

So many emotions. I don't want to be trapped here like this, vulnerable with a man that clearly despises me. However, a part of me, some disgusting part of me that's no doubt completely hormone related, enjoys it. My world is engulfed in his expensive musky cologne, and fresh cotton clothes. His eyes are what do it for that traitorous part of me the most, those sexy smouldering silver eyes.

Finally, sense snaps back into me, like a bucket of cold water. I push him away as hard as I can, he doesn't move much, he just laughs at my attempt which only makes me angrier. He moves out of my space and tucks his hands into his checked trouser pockets, the most human gesture I think I've seen him do.

"Stay the fuck away from me." I mean to say it reasonably quiet but of course it comes out in an embarrassing shriek. I gather myself and run, as fast as humanly possible, ignoring his booming laughter, back the way I came, towards the next form of torture this school has to offer- Debutant Lessons.

Chapter 7:

I hurl myself through the classroom door, all eyes turn to me as it slams shut behind me. I bite my lip as I try not to look fazed by the sneer of the teacher standing at the front of the class, I scan the group of haughty looking girls for Cora and I force my feet to move as I spot her sitting at the front. I flick back my hair and smooth down my dress, as I walk into the make-shift tea party.

"Jesus Lou, what the fuck?" she whispers as everyone's heads turn back to the front.

"I'll explain at lunch," I say, quickly grabbing my notebook. I try and focus on the words coming from the teachers mouth, fuck I don't even know her name... My grip on my pencil tightens as I spiral into a Grenville rabbit hole. *Who does this entitled prick think he is? Why does he think shoving me against a wall and almost kissing me is acceptable behaviour? Did he try to kiss me? Or did I read that completely wrong? Well, now I know his game and won't be caught off guard again- that's for sure. Why does he hate me so much? He treats me like I stabbed one of his relatives.*

"Louisa, can *you* tell me?" The sharp voice from the teacher cuts through my thoughts like a knife. A cold sweep of dread falls over me as I realise I haven't been listening at all. I blink, wracking my brain to see if my subconscious remembers anything that Bella had taught me last night, but now too much time has passed and I can't think of a single thing to mutter back. Great start to a first day...

"I'm sorry Professor, I'm very new to all of this stuff so I'm not sure of the answer." Mainly the truth...

Her lips curl into a viscous smile, "My name is Lady Elena, you will address me as My Lady. Which is the customary way to greet someone of my status. Had you arrived on time today, you would have known that. Can you step up here to the front please, Louisa?"

My face turns a shade of beetroot as I stand, my chair making a scraping noise across the floor, Lady Elena's eye twitches at the sound. Was I not supposed to do that?

I walk up to the front and stand in the spot where she'd gestured, picking a painting of a black snake hidden among a bouquet of beautiful white roses on the back wall to stare at.

"Now ladies, here is a good example of how to know when to cut your losses during the courting season. Louisa here needs to become a lady, but she has a number of factors working against her." I want the ground to swallow me up as the sniggers erupt from the girls in the room. "Her hair, while the colour isn't awful- the cut is. An easy fix, do you agree?" They nod their heads in unison, like the perfect little robots they are.

I stare at the painting, determined not to give this woman the satisfaction of breaking me. It's just like Professor Daphne had warned, but I'm sure this woman is just warming up.

"Her clothes, a perfect example of why we have stylists. This beautiful dress has been made to look like it's straight off the rack, and not imported from Italy. Which is tough to do might I add" More sniggers. "All of these things on the outside, we can change, yes? But her accent? Her mannerisms? Her mind? I'm not so sure, so do I waste all of my efforts trying to change a man? Or find another suitor to spend my time with? Remember ladies, you only have a few hours a week with the man you're courting. These physical attributes in a man need to be zeroed in on as quickly as you can. Time is precious... especially, my time."

Of course this place still has courting, it's like I'm on another planet. Then again inbreeding has always worked for the royal family, so why wouldn't the elite keep their dating circle small too.

"See me after the lesson has finished."

She dismisses me with a wave of her perfectly polished hand, I walk back to my seat sheepishly as the whispering starts again. I grab my pencil and write down another thing I need to research- courting.

My blood runs cold as I finish the word, I don't remember putting the package into my bag... My brother's package is in the hands of Benjamin Grenville...

My head pounds and my body aches as we leave the classroom. Who would've thought learning not to scrape your tea spoon on a cup and walking in heels with books on your head would be so draining? These little habits would have been insignificant if my Dad's prison sentence didn't ride on me turning into a lady. I spend the entire time it takes us to walk out onto the grounds moping, trying to figure out how I'm going to get this package back from him. Today has been a total shit show and it's only what? 12pm? I kind of hope that nothing else unexpected gets thrown at me today.

"Why are you so clammy?" Bella sneers at me over her salad.

I flip her the middle finger and toss my hair behind my shoulder,

"What is it?" Cora's brows furrow. I chewed my food slowly, wondering if I could trust them. Definitely not with the whole truth- but enough that I could maybe gain some insight into the puzzling heir of the university.

"Can you honestly say, hand on heart, that I can trust the two of you?" I narrow my eyes at them, studying their reactions.

"You're not the only one who has to get this right, we both have a lot to personally gain from having a friendship with you. It's a bonus that we find you tolerable so far, but we want to help you. So whatever it is that's got your knickers in a twist, spill it." I bite my lip as I take in Bella's words, at least she's being transparent. Yes this is a forced friendship, but does it really matter what their motivations are for wanting me to succeed if it means I actually do?

"Fine, I keep having these... run-ins with Benjamin Grenville. And today I'm fairly certain he was about to kiss me." I keep my eyes down on my food, pushing the cold pasta I'd made that morning around with my fork.

"Are you fucking serious?" I finally look up as Bella shouts, earning a slap on the arm from Cora.

"Keep your voice down." She whispers.

"Okay, we're going to need context here because Benjamin Grenville is not someone you just get involved with by chance. His family is the most calculating, power hungry..."

"Yes, okay. I get it. Grenville bad." I hold up my hand to stop Bella's rant.

I tell them everything- apart from my brother's favour- I tell them about how just a look from him sets my skin on fire, how that fire had started at the ball and his threat. I leave out the part where I almost planted my lips on his as he had me pinned against the wall...

Finally when I'm done, I look between my unlikely friends as they smirk at one another.

"He's got under your skin." Bella accuses, pointing her fork in my direction before scoffing her face with a bit of shredded carrot. I shake my head.

"I tell you that the most powerful man here hates my guts and is stalking me, and you tell me he's got under my skin?" I ask, utterly dumbfounded at her accusation. I look to Cora for moral support but she gives me a sly grin.

"Daphne's going to love this." Her eyebrow twitches at me.

"Why would I tell Professor Daphne?" Curiosity dances on my tongue.

"Because the whole point of her experiment is to create the ultimate weapon against the most powerful men in the country?" she says as if I'm stupid.

"I don't want to be a weapon," I say it under my breath so the students walking by won't catch wind of our conversation.

"What *do* you want Lou? You can't sit here and tell me that this wouldn't be hugely advantageous to you. Besides, he is undeniably gorgeous. I don't think it would be too much of a chore for you to wrap your legs around a stunning face like that" Bella pops a grape into her mouth as her and Cora giggle between each other, I shake my head and hide my blushing face.

"Courting starts next week and if you play your cards right you could end the season with the richest fucking man in here." My mind reels at the possibility, before the self doubt creeps in. Why would someone like him be interested in me?

"I don't want to court *anyone* or be a debutante. I'm here to learn, to better myself and make a difference in the world. I'm only agreeing to Daphne's terms because I need these qualifications." Before I give too much away, Cora's eyes widen and she makes a face at something, or should I say someone, approaching us. I turn and place my hand over my eyes to shield them from the sun. I don't know who I'm expecting to appear in front of me, but Sebastian walking over to me in full polo gear is not on today's bingo card.

"Louisa, I was hoping to catch you," he says as he stops just a little way from where we're sitting. "I'm sure the girls are getting you up to speed on how courting works?"

Bella and Cora stifle laughs and I blush at his advance. I peek behind him to see he's with a group of men, also in full polo gear, one of them with icy blonde hair... I can't tell if he's looking over or can even hear me, I give Sebastian my best flirty smile.

"Sebastian, so wonderful of you to join us. Will you sit? Or do you have somewhere more important to be?" by the glimmer in his eyes, he doesn't miss the flirtatious edge to my tone. I remember my lessons from earlier and I hold out my hand for him to kiss, he gives an approving look as he does.

Nailed it.

"How could I not stop when three beauties lie between me and the polo field. Will you be watching the rugby game in a few weeks? We've got Oxford coming up here of all people, they're due a good thrashing." His white teeth flash in the sun, which I'm sure would be dazzling to the average woman who hasn't had the pleasure of Grenville pinning them against a wall.

"I'd be delighted." Sebastian beams at my response, like I've just made his week.

"I'll save you a seat in my box," he says, as he walks backwards towards his friends. My eyes, however, can't help but flicker over to the tall blonde behind him. I'm cursing the sun right now because it's impossible to get a good look at his reaction from the encounter.

"I hope you know what you're doing there." Bella smirks and I give her a coy smug, wondering where my confidence has come from all of a sudden.

"Let the games begin ladies." Cora says in approval.

On my way back to my room, the day finally over, I replay all the information that the girls have unknowingly given me. *So Daphne wants to turn me into a weapon? But how? What could I possibly offer these rich men in comparison to any other woman here? I'm not well bred, yes my family has influence but thats for all of the wrong reasons... What's the end game with these people?*

No matter how hard I work my brain, I can't grasp the answers, so I focus on replaying the politics lesson from earlier instead. I give myself a mental note to head to the Library after dinner tonight, there's a formal one that takes place here most evenings but right now I've no interest in that.

When I finally head into my room to dump my stuff, I'm surprised to find the package from my brother waiting for me on the kitchen counter. What the fuck? How did he get in here? More importantly... why did he return it?

My stomach fills with dread as I rip off the silver bow he'd tied round it and look inside, despite my brother's warning. To my relief, it's just a phone. A very old phone, but a phone nonetheless. Pulling mine out, I call Frankie right away. He picks up after the second ring.

"Why have you sent me a phone?" I ask, I'm in no mood to dance around it anymore. He can give me answers at least.

"Baby sister, I thought I told you not to look in there." He breathes out a long breath and I can tell he's smoking again.

"Well there were some... complications. I had to make sure it wasn't tampered with."

He laughs at my excuse like it's a lie.

"I knew you wouldn't be able to resist. Right, at midnight in a few weeks time that phone's going to ring. Don't answer it. Just head straight to the main gate and-"

"Woah, hang on there! What the fuck do you think you're doing? I don't want you here, Frankie! If I find out you're even so much as in the same county as me, I'll kill you myself."

He sighs at the threat, the sound of his burning cigarette coming through so clearly, it's like I'm there with him.

"I fucked up, Lou. I'm in some deep shit and I need you to do this for me or else I'm dead." I shift on the balls of my feet at the sudden tone change.

"What's happened? What kind of trouble?" I ask, my mind whirring trying to think of a logical way out of whatever shit he's gotten himself into.

"We got raided, we had a rat in the ranks. The stupid fuckers couldn't tie us to anything, they didn't have enough evidence but the heats on us right now. I can't be seen doing what I normally do. I'm not even in brum right now." He sounds exhausted.

"But just because the heat's on us right now, doesn't mean that Oscar stops expecting payment." The name sends shivers down my spine, *fucking Oscar…*

"So pick up the package, sell what's in there for me to all those stupidly rich friends of yours and we'll all sleep better at night knowing Oscar gets his money and stays away from us."

I can do this for him, just this once.

"I'll do one shipment but after that, you're on your own. There's too many eyes on me here…"

His laugh is humourless.

"They didn't just threaten mum this time, they threatened you too. Oscar knows where you are, it was his idea to get you to distribute for us. You know I want to keep you out of this, but he's got us by throat right now until the pigs fuck off." He takes one last drag of his cigarette, "Thank you Lou, I'll text the details." He hangs up, leaving me to wonder how Oscar knew where to find me.

Chapter 8:

The weeks fly by in a blink and I welcome the mild chill that October brings. Between debutant training and trying to wrap my head around the advanced classes; I spend most of my down time pouring over books.

The girls have been busy over analysing my encounter with Grenville, but I've been focusing on avoiding the shit out of him these last few weeks. Which hasn't been hard, I'm told that instead of attending usual lessons, Men 'hold council' together in a different section in the university... Basically they spend hours measuring each other's dicks. *The sexism in this place makes my skin crawl.*

The only times I've seen him are when he does that irritating thing of sitting in front of me during politics so I can't see. I practically know every crevice of the back of his head at this point. As much as I wanted to, I didn't approach him to say thanks for returning the parcel undamaged. I tell myself it's the least he could do after invading my space like that.

I regret sleeping in the moment I come out of my room. Bella and Cora are already up and dressed like super models as they discuss tonight's rugby game in depth.

"Jesus Lou, you look like shit."

I give her a sarcastic smile, if only she knew the bags under my eyes were because I was up half the night panicking about the incoming shipment coming from Oscar today. My anxiety spiked a few days ago when Frankie had texted me the details of where and when to meet the delivery boy. At least Oscar wasn't coming himself.

"Here, we got you this," Cora says, flinging a black t-shirt at me.

I unfold it to see the words "Grenville University" in candy apple red writing complete with the crow coat of arms beneath it. I lift an eyebrow.

"I'm not wearing this," I say as I throw the t-shirt back.

"Wow you suddenly give a shit what you look like? We must be rubbing off on you..." They giggle together, reminding me of a group of mean girls from secondary school.

"Are you both wearing them?" I say with a sigh.

"Yes! It's tradition for the debutants to be the ultimate cheerleaders." Cora beams at me, it seems like she's genuinely excited for today's match.

"But we did get you this to go with that." Bella reaches behind her and pulls out the most stunning black designer bag.

I fold my arms, determined not to be bribed by it, it calls out to me as the little golden key chain dangling from it jingles. *Damn you Bella.*

"Don't give me that sad puppy face, I saw you eyeing mine the other day- consider it an official induction into our inner circle." Bella smiles and jingles it a little more.

"Oh, so you're saying you aren't just friends with me because some scary professor threatened your inheritance if you refused? Aww, I love this sentimental side of you." I say sarcastically as I snatch the bag eagerly from her hands.

This bag has been in my dreams for about a year. The first time I saw it was while I was working in the corner shop near our flat, Sharon from the street over had managed to get her hands on some decent knock offs from Turkey and all of the girls were wearing them. When I saw the real thing on Bella, I got the same feeling. Like I was a little girl again picking outfits for my Barbie's at the toy shop. I'm surprised she'd noticed that it piqued my interest. Perhaps I don't give her enough credit for how observant she really is.

"Tonight's more about the after party anyway," Cora says. "It'll be in the observatory tonight as the sky's meant to be clear." She's definitely excited.

"What time does the party start?" *Please don't say midnight.*

"Around 10 after the formal meal, I hear Oxford are staying on their tour bus tonight. How delicious." Bella mumbles as she takes a sip of her tea.

"I heard the captain's a bit of a dish. It'll do me good to get my hands on some fresh meat." I wince as Cora kicks Bella in the shin with her pointed white stiletto.

"If you mention him again I'll puncture your eye with these," she says to her playfully as she takes off the shoe and waves it near her face. To Bella's credit she doesn't flinch. I decide not to pry into whatever drama surrounds Cora. I busy myself, making some poached eggs and toast, only half listening to their gossiping behind me.

At least the party starts early enough that I won't be missed when I go to pick up the shipment. I look down at my arms to see goosebumps appearing on my pale skin, I really hope Oscar doesn't deliver it himself. Although knowing that sadistic asshole, he probably will.

When I'm done piecing my breakfast together, I set it down next to the girls and try my best to look engaged in their conversation. I smile and nod at the correct times, give my opinion if it's asked but on the inside, I'm plagued with anxiety about tonight. When I'm done, I tell them I'm going to get dressed and head to the library for a few hours before the match starts, but of course this is met with grumbles about manicures and hair care. I shrug them off because I know I need to be in my own head right now. I need to formulate a plan and then a back up plan and then a back up back up plan... Oscar is not the type of man you want to piss off and if my brother is in as deep shit as he says, I have to prepare for the worst.

I'm quick to shower and get ready, but I do manage to have a coffee and persuade Cora to braid my hair into two very neat french plaits.

The best thing about Cora is that I don't feel the need to fill the silence when I'm around her. I can sit comfortably and almost be myself, but with Bella? It's like I need to constantly be thinking of a snarky retort for a comment she's going to make. I know her sharp tongue is just a defence mechanism but we're not close enough yet to have a deep conversation about it.

When I finally walk through the doors of the library, I'm greeted with the comforting smell of books. *This is what home feels like.* No matter how many times I walk in here, I'll never get over the scale of the place. Every inch is covered in books, from the black and white tiled floor to the high arches of the ceiling, the never-ending maze of bookcases send me a siren call. I'm not here to study or work on an assignment, I just need the comfort, a distraction from the fact my evening will be consumed with selling drugs on campus. So I pick up my feet and delve into the depths of the decaying tomes, searching for anything that will dampen my anxiety.

I find myself in a section I've not discovered yet. I glance up at the sign hanging down in the middle of the aisle to try and get my bearings, "War" it reads. How cheerful. I carry on, wondering how far back I am to the exit when I hear hushed voices coming from a few aisles away. I know I shouldn't but I creep a little closer. Whatever they're saying sounds like an argument, but why are they all the way back here?

"You'll do exactly as I say, out of respect to this family." It's an older gentleman, his accent is thick and posh like the rest of them here but I don't recognise it. Perhaps a Professor I haven't met yet.

"I'd rather gouge my eyes out with a desert spoon than waste another moment in this pathetic place, *father*."

Now that voice I know, although Grenvilles tone is nothing more than utter boredom, you can feel the poison lacing it. His dad is here? Why are they in the back of the library? Why are they arguing?

Then I look up, the answer right in front of me, swinging gently on a ghostly wind as it hangs above the aisles. "The History of Grenville."

THE HOUSE OF GRENVILLE

"This is my price, if you refuse to pay it, you leave me with no choice. I'll expose you if you don't do as I wish."

Woah, blackmail? Grenville's laugh is cold and lifeless as he lowers his voice to barely a whisper.

"If you don't bite your tongue, I'll rip it out from your throat. I will not have you try to black mail me when..."

Holy shit. I lean in just a little bit closer to... *Fuck.* I lean a little too hard, and the books fall into the opposite aisle creating a gap in the shelf. It goes quiet, and I hold my breath as I dare to peek through only to find furious silver eyes staring right back at me.

I do whatever a perfectly normal person would do, and run, as quickly and quietly as I can out of the library. As soon as I'm out in the corridor and think I can breathe for a second, I hear the door open behind me again. I don't look back. I just keep running. I don't even know where I'm running to, but I hear his footsteps. He's catching up with me quickly. I skid a little as I turned the corner, ignoring the other students gaping at me. I reach a dead end, so I decide to do the most unladylike thing in the fucking world and vault out of the open window next to me into the round courtyard that leads out to the gardens.

As I launch myself from the window sill, my foot slips on the damn rain covering it, sending me flying towards the ground. I fall straight on my arse, and smack my head on the concrete as I land. The pain is blinding, and for a split second, everything is blurry. I reach up to touch my head, I can't feel any bleeding, thank god. I need to get off of this floor before he finds out where I've gone.

A pale hand appears in front of me, outstretched for me to take. He's got me right where he wants me. I don't take it, instead I narrow my eyes at cool demeanor, like he didnt just chase me through the fucking building, and pick myself up.

"Can I help you?" I ask, daring him to make a scene in front of the audience we've gathered.

"I saw you fall, I came to check if you're alright." His tone is… friendly. But I don't miss the threat lurking within his eyes. I glance around and there are a lot of people watching this little interaction. This must be why he's playing nice, to protect his reputation. If he picks a fight with me here, everyone would want to know what it was about and why I'd fallen out of a window. Then they would have to find out that I was actually running from him, he was hunting me down because of what I'd heard…

"I think it's best that we take you to get checked out, you look terribly confused. Please let me escort you."

I scramble back from him, like a cornered animal. This guy just threatened to rip out his Dad's tongue, I'm not going anywhere with him.

He cocks an eyebrow and does that stupid thing with his tongue that ignites something in me. So I hesitantly reach out and take his arm, regretting it the instant I do as he leans down and whispers, "Good girl." I shiver as his breath grazes my neck, but I don't miss the malice in his voice.

We walk through the crowd, and I keep my eyes fixed on the floor. Wondering exactly what the fuck I should do now.

Chapter 9:

"It's bad enough you follow me around like some flea ridden dog, but now you must listen in to my every conversation? Whatever disgusting state school you attended clearly didn't teach you any manners." Grenvilles grip tightens on my arm as spits the words at me in a hushed voice.

I snatch my arm away from his and slap him hard across the face.

"How dare you? You're the one stalking me and making my life a living hell. Don't you have anything better to do than this playground bullshit? I'm here to better myself so that I can actually make a difference to my family's lives, not that you would ever understand the concept of working hard with that silver spoon up your arse!" He swipes his fingers delicately across the bottom of his perfectly chiselled jaw.

"You are an infuriating woman. I caught you in the forbidden section of MY library and now have the audacity to accuse me of stalking you?" My cheeks flush as he closes the distance between us, my heart pounds in my ears as his face moves towards mine.

"You chase me through the school like a hound from hell and now you want me to apologise?!"

"Do not pretend to know what it is that I want, Garrick." He whispers as he rests his forehead against mine, his breath mingles with my own as his hands cup each side of my face. The foreign softness of his touch makes me tense.

"What are you doing?" My voice breaks as I speak and my hands shake at my side. *This is dangerous territory.*

"What I want." His thumb grazes my bottom lip as he searches my eyes for permission, I give him a hesitant nod. *If curiosity killed the cat, I'm sure there could be worse ways to die.*

I never take my eyes off his as he leans in again, and neither does he. When his lips meet mine, it sparks an inferno inside of me. The kiss is hateful and passionate, I lose myself in the moment and dig my nails into his arms.

"Mr Grenville, courting does not start until next week. It's inappropriate for you to be seen so publicly with Miss Garrick." *Shit.* My stomach drops as Professor Daphne's voice carries over towards me. He breaks away the kiss leaving me dazed and confused,

"Apologies Professor, I'll be sure to conduct myself in an appropriate manner from now on." He doesn't take his eyes off mine, I watch a glimmer of a silent plea beneath his cold exterior. I frown at him, It's like this planned out exactly how he wanted it to. The thought should terrify me, but it doesn't.

"You do understand the implications of such a public display, don't you Mr Grenville?"

Implications? She walks slowly towards us and I finally tear my eyes away from him. Daphne looks like she belongs on the cover of French Vogue, and as her eyes travel down my outfit lingering on my swollen lips- guilt and shame washes over me. The entire university will know about this before the sun sets. I would have proved all of their whispers right. That I was here to bag myself a rich husband and get out of the smoke filled city.

"Yes, I do, Professor. I'll be making my public declaration tonight at the Rugby match, in order to protect my own and Miss Garricks reputation." He lifts my chin up with his index finger, so I have no choice but to look at him again.

"A public declaration?" she says slyly, moving closer towards us.

"What can I say, Miss Garrick has me entranced." His eyes flicker back down to my lips and my treacherous body floods with need.

"Very well Mr Grenville, I'll ensure Miss Garrick is fully prepared. I'd like to see you before the game with Corinthia and Belladonna Miss Garrick, I have time now if you're... done with Mr. Grenville?"

Her tone grabs my attention, her smile tells me everything I need to know. Her plans for me now involve Grenville, my stomach twists.

"Yes, um, I have time now." I slide myself out from between him and the wall I didn't know I was pressed up against, towards Professor Daphne. I shiver, my body suddenly cold from the loss of his.

"I'll see you at the game," I mutter to him sheepishly as he plasters on that smirk I loathe and walks away without another word.

Professor Daphne gives me a look of approval and we walk towards her office in silence. My phone buzzes in my back pocket and just like that, reality hits me. I have bigger fish to fry, how could I let myself get so wrapped up in this man?

I notice that It's not my normal phone that's buzzing, and it's incessant. Cold dread washes over me as I slyly pull out the burner phone. The name from my nightmares flashes on the screen. *Oscar.*

WE REACH THE OFFICE and I find the girls are already there, looking as confused as I feel. I take the empty seat in between them.

"Are you both aware that Benjamin Grenville intends to make a public declaration for Louisa this evening at the rugby game?" She asks them with a smile that would make a cheshire cat jealous.

"The fuck Lou?! I told you he's not someone you want to fuck around with." Cora's eyes are wide with. I shrink down in my seat feeling like a child being scolded.

"I'm just as surprised as you all are." I huff out, trying to push away the anxiety of seeing Oscar's name.

"I caught them kissing in the hallway by the courtyard. You were seen by at least six or seven others before I came around the corner. Do you have any idea the damage you've done to your image? Declarations are not supposed to happen until after weeks of chaperoned dates," she leans back in her chair, excitement lacing her features. I realise then it's the most human action I've ever seen her do. A tiny crack in her perfectly poised persona.

"He's declaring for you?! Professor, you cannot let this happen. If this happens, he'll own her." I look at Bella, confused at her reaction.

"Own me? What do you mean?" I ask, looking between the three of them.

"You stupid naive girl, he's Benjamin Grenville- his family basically owns the United Kingdom. There isn't a single pie that family doesn't have their hands in, getting involved with him is quite possibly the stupidest thing you could've done here." I blush from the sting of her words,

"I didn't mean to, that's not what happened." My voice breaks again but I regain my composure quickly.

"Stop whining, Louisa, own your actions," Professor Daphne spits at me.

"This is indeed the stupidest yet most brilliant situation you could have put us in. I will help you out of this, if being owned by him isn't something you want. But you'll have to go to hell and back to pull this off.." I glance between the girls, they both look hesitant to trust Professor Daphne, but what choice do I have? We're all in this together, and I still have a prison sentence to reduce.

Chapter 10:

"Can you please just say something Lou? Because you've been staring into space for the last half an hour."

I hear the words, but don't process them. I don't remember walking back from Professor Daphne's office. I don't remember how I came to have a steaming hot cup of tea put in my hands.

"I'm sorry, I was just trying to figure out how the fuck I'm going to pull this off." I mutter before sipping the tea,I sigh as the warmth of it brings me back to life.

"Oh bore off Lou, you already have the bloke by the balls you may as well crush them while they're in your hands." I give a humourless "Ha-Ha" to Bella as I narrow my eyes at her.

"He despises me. I don't understand why he said what he said earlier and now I have to go along with it and play the happy little stepford wife, so that I can spy on his stupid political party?" I'm just met with an eye roll from Bella, so I look to Cora for support instead.

"He obviously likes you, why is that so hard for you to believe? He kissed you- in a public place which is a massive no-no! Why else would he declare for you like that? What other explanation could there possibly be? If for whatever reason that's not it, then take your opportunity for revenge, crush his balls as Bella says."

I sit with that thought for a moment, could that actually be the answer? That he just likes me? Had a moment of weakness and now wants to protect my reputation? The man is an arse hole, an attractive one but he's made me feel like utter shit since coming here. Maybe revenge isn't so far-fetched, I could certainly have some fun with this.

"What's his instagram handle?" I snatch my phone from my back pocket.

"I've actually got his number here if you just want to text him and not be a total psychopath," Bella drawls, holding her own phone out for me to see.

My pulse threatens to burst from my neck, but I decide I deserve to have a fuck it moment. I type his number into my phone, and start typing furiously.

"Grenville, you better have a reasonable explanation for all of this. Please do not declare yourself (or whatever the fuck it is you pompous pricks do around here) at the match. I want nothing to do with you," I read it out loud before I send it and they both cringe. "What's wrong with it? I think that sounds good. Assertive." I look between the pair of them, utter bemusement plastered across their faces.

"Don't tell him not to do it, you idiot. Use that oddly logical brain of yours, see this through until it doesn't benefit you anymore. It's not like you have to marry him, Daphne never said anything about that."

"No, I just have to find a way to dismantle his political party from the inside or else I'll lose my scholarship here?" I retort with dripping sarcasm.

"Oo, I know- let's have some champagne and write a list of pros and cons? That helped me decide where to take my gap year." Cora beams and Bella and I roll our eyes at her golden retriever attitude.

"Fine, you two sit in your own misery. I'm going to get ready and make sure I'm so drunk that I don't recognise my ex boyfriend."

Now I really feel like a bad friend, here I am worrying about my pathetic dramas but I haven't even asked her what the deal is with this Oxford bloke.

"How about I don't make a decision until he declares for me and we all get royally pissed?" I say trying to lighten Cora's dampened mood. She nods a little too enthusiastically. I shove my phone into my pocket and begin the chaos that is- getting ready.

As Bella cracks open our third bottle of champagne, I instantly regret not eating today. My stomach growls as I get up to make some food. The stylists and makeup artists have taken over most of the space in the living area, so I try my best to weave in between them all and not get in the way. I start pulling out pots and pans when a knock at the door sends the giggling into silence. I look at Bella but wiggles her freshly painted fingers at me. I sigh and walk over to the door, rollers still pinned in my hair and my pink bunny slippers sliding across the floor.

Swinging it open, I find none other than Benjamin Grenville leaning in my doorway. I give him an icy glare and grit my teeth. "What do you want?" I say as quietly as I can.

He smirks and pushes his arm off the doorway, the motion dragging my attention to his Rugby kit. My god, how did I not notice how fit this guy is? I don't think I've ever seen such muscle definition in a bicep before.

"If you're done ogling..."

Shit! I look back up at him trying not to remember how his lips felt against mine, or his body, or anything remotely pleasant about this man.

"I've come to talk about that delightful text message you sent me." He gives me a grin that could rival the Devil's as the colour drains from my face.

"I didn't send you a text." Did I? I typed it out then shoved it back into my pocket. Oh balls.

He cocks an eyebrow which means he can see right through me,

"Well, I meant it. Don't bother with your bullshit, I know it's not real anyway." The words spill out before I can catch them.

"Do you want them to be real?" His eyebrows knit together slightly.

"No, I don't, I want nothing to do with you" I say as I fold my arms across my chest.

"Well, that's too bad." He scratches the back of head.

"I brought you some food, I know you didn't get to eat earlier because of our... indiscretion and I knew you'd want to drink before becoming the talk of the campus." He gestures behind him to reveal a skinny, tall man, with dark hair, dressed in a chef's uniform. He nods at me slightly as he walks past me into our room.

"What the fuck? Are you... is this some sort of apology?" This man confuses me to no end. His eyes harden, all traces of humour lost. We're back to that now then.

"Why don't you stop asking questions and just say thank you?"

"If you think I'm going into this ridiculous... *Thing*...Without questions, then you've picked the wrong girl to fuck around with." We stare at each other for a moment, both of us wondering who will be the first to back down. He licks his lips as he looks me up and down.

"Make sure you look your best, there's going to be photographers at the game." His eyebrows rise as he glances down at my slippers and I roll my eyes as he turns on his heel and walks away.

"Thank you!" I shout after him, trying not to admire how great his arse looks in those shorts. I slam the door shut and stand there for a moment. "What a fucking prick, who does he think..." I trail off as I turn back around to see I have an audience.

"Well that went well." Bella says, holding out another glass of champagne for me.

Chapter 11:

We cut through the courtyard, surrounded by a sea of students. The vibe is sky high and honestly I'm not mad about it. Looking around, I'm pretty sure everyone is already half cut and it's nice to see everyone's perfect masks falter a little bit. *Good to know I'm surrounded by humans and not robots.* Even Bella is a little more loose this evening, she's still her usual poised self but there's a spring in her step. It seems like the only person who doesn't want to be here is Cora. She doesn't even try to hide her anxiety as she fiddles endlessly with her hair as we walk down together arm-in-arm.

This is what I imagined University to be like, a bunch of young adults discovering themselves by doing stupid shit. I push my own dramas to the back of my mind, promising myself to deal with it all once the time comes as we finally make it out to the pitch.

Of course this place has its own stadium. Complete with the bright lights that cost at least £100,000 each, not to mention the enormous flat screen slap bang in the middle of the stands. I suddenly feel like an idiot for thinking it would be on a plain old field.

As we approach the doors and are patted down by security, Bella gives our names and we're escorted to the front row.

"Wow, these seats are great- thank you Bella!" I say as we take our seats.

"Oh, these aren't courtesy of the 'Belladonna Fortune.'" She smirks. "These are reserved for the Greenville's," she whispers to me and my eyes almost pop out of my head.

"I need another drink," I say with a laugh, a genuine laugh that feels alien to me.

"Aren't these seats reserved for his family?" I ask, scanning around us in case we get rounded on by a disgruntled family member of his.

"No, Grenville Senior sits in the box up there." I follow her finger up to the large glass box next to the big screen. It's got some kind of protective film over the glass that doesn't let you see in, but other people can see out. How secretive...

"Excuse me, you're in my seat." A high pitched shrill voice comes from our right and I turn and see a very tall, very thin blonde girl clutching an expensive brown embossed handbag. She's wearing enormous sunglasses despite the fact the sun has almost set. The stranger has that same sort of snooty air about her, but whereas Bella and Cora look like they belong on the cover of Vogue- this girl looks like she's straight out of a teen magazine that promotes Anorexia as a fashion trend.

I have no idea who she is and I don't remember seeing her in any of my lectures. I glance at Cora, but she's already stood up with her mean girl face on.

"Becca Tamworth, I wondered when you'd show that ugly face of yours. I heard you didn't take it very well when you were assigned to Oxford and not here." Cora cocks her eyebrow daring her to make a move. Becca snatches off her sunglasses and purses her large lips at us. *Jesus this is like some kind of cowboy stand off.*

"These seats are reserved for Grenville guests and she is sitting in mine." She looks me up and down like I'm a piece of shit, so I throw her my best Birmingham glare.

"Who are you anyway?" She sneers, "I don't remember seeing you at any of our party's before."

"She's a guest of the Grenville's, now bore off before I undo all the hard work your plastic surgeon put into your new nose."

I snort at Bella's response, earning a quick once over from Becca before she stalks off like a toddler having a tantrum.

"Who the fuck was that?" I ask under my breath.

"That's Grenville's ex-girlfriend, at least I think they were official. It was all very hush hush, but I know their parents are close."

A wave of insecurity threatens to dampen my mood.. Of course this guy had ex girlfriends. Was blonde his type? Should I dye my hair?

"Don't let her get in your head, there's a reason you're sitting here and not her."

I nod at Cora's words and squeeze her hand as she takes mine.

"We've got you Lou, we won't let anything happen to you," Bella says as she takes my other hand. I squeeze it and smile back at them both, that ugly feeling of jealousy washing away.

"Enough soppiness, the game is about to start," Bella says as she pats down some of the frizz that has formed on my curls. "Are you ready Lou?".

"Yes, I've made up my mind." Just as I say it I feel my phone vibrate in my bag that's laid on top of my feet. I pull it out and open it up, my heart skipping as I read the text from the unknown number.

"I'll explain everything at the party tonight, please just go with it until then. I'm sorry about earlier." Wow, an actual apology from the man. I want to text something sarcastic back but my mind is reeling, instead I show the text to the girls and they giggle between each other.

"Quickly text him back, it starts in a moment!" Cora Is like a giddy school girl and I'm glad her mood seems to have lifted.

"Be sexy and dramatic," Bella suggests.

I think for a moment and then type three little words that I secretly hope makes his stomach flip upside down. "I'm all yours."

The girls watch me type and send it.

"Wow, didn't know you had it in you, Garrick. Well played!" Bella says as she digs through her bag.

The phone vibrates in my hand and I open it a little too eagerly,

"Good Girl. ;)"

My cheeks heat as I try not to melt at his words. I don't have a chance to settle my nerves as music echoes from the speakers and the commentator begins his speech.

"Welcome students, for our first game of the season- Oxford VS Grenville!" The crowd cheers and so do we. I find myself getting caught up in the electric atmosphere, I've never been to a rugby match before. My family was always more football oriented. The teams enter the pitch from opposite sides of the field, the Grenville students around me start booing the Oxford boys in blue. Our black and red uniform stands out magnificently against the green field.

My heart stutters when I spot him a mile away, his unusually light hair a striking contrast to the rest of dark haired men that surround him. Even though we're in the front it's still hard to make out little details with the pitch being so big, but I don't miss how toned his body is. I let my mind wander to what it would be like for him to own me, it couldn't be so bad right? Yes he was a total arsehole, but he was also gorgeous, smart, I bet he's funny too if he were to let you get close enough to see that side of him.

I scream and cheer with the others- for the first time surrendering myself completely to the allure of my surroundings. Perhaps even to him. I'm not stupid, I know there is a huge possibility that he doesn't like me in that way at all. So I won't get ahead of myself. But just for now, I'll pretend he's mine.

As I watch him jog across the field, his short hair bouncing and thigh muscles clenching with each stride, I think about how easy it would be to fall for him. The teams line up in the middle and begin their chant of the national anthem, pledging themselves to our monarch. I watch the big screen as the camera pans to each member of the teams, all strikingly good looking.

Bella hands me a paper cup filled with a liquid that smells like spiced cinnamon and rum. I drink it a little greedily and savour the warmth it gives me against the October chill. I glance up at the sky, the men's voices still booming. The sun has set completely now, the stars twinkling, clear and bright, I never saw through the Birmingham fog growing up.

I feel at peace. I'm here with my friends laughing and joking under the stars, at the university of my dreams, at a rugby game full of hot boys! I could take the embarrassment and belittlement in the classes, I could keep working extra hard in the library if it meant I could stay here and feel like this.

My bubble bursts as the singing stops and something crimson catches my attention from the corner of my eye. My stomach drops at the sight of him, at the sight of Frankie smoking, beaten and bloody. The light from the stands bouncing off the golden chain hanging from his neck. I push past Bella and make my way over to him as quickly as I can without drawing too much attention. When I reach him, I see the damage.

We say nothing as we fall back into our routine from home, I examine his busted lip and nose. He smokes and gazes off moodily. Old habits die hard, I guess. It dawns on me then… Why would he come here?

"I told you to answer the phone," he says roughly.

"The only person that's rang me is him, you know I won't deal with him directly," I say as I lift up his blood soaked shirt discreetly, trying to determine where the blood is coming from. On his right side there's a deep cut, not enough to be fatal but he's still bleeding and I don't know how long it's been since this fight.

"You're going to bleed out, we need to get you to a hospital," I mutter, glancing around to make sure nobody's looking at us, thankfully everyone's too engrossed in the game.

"Lou, who the fuck is this and why is he covered in blood?" Cora appears from nowhere behind me.

"Shit, Cora, this is Frankie, my older brother." I make a quick and hasty introduction as I try to figure out where the fuck I'm going to take him.

"He was mugged on the way here. He came to drop off a package for me from home." The lie comes easy and fast and I flash him a warning look to play along. He gives Cora his signature "Lady killer" smirk which earns an eye roll from me.

"Don't worry, love, you should see the other guy."

"Oh my god how dreadful! Lou, you need to take your seat, the match started. I can take care of your brother if you like? I can't stand to look at my ex for a moment longer if I'm honest."

I think about her proposition for a moment as I glance back towards the pitch, I'm wary of the secrets Frankie might divulge about my past. But then again, it's only an hour and then I can go to him and find out exactly what happened.

I nod reluctantly and run through what to do and where my first aid kit is. She tells me not to come back until after the party, but I shake my head and explain that he will need stitches. Cora grimaces at the thought. I stay rooted to the spot, watching as she supports his weight, I pray silently to god that he keeps his mouth shut.

"I'll explain everything later, let's just get this declaration over with," I mutter to Bella as I take my seat. My palms sweat as the anxiety settles back in, I keep my eye on the enormous clock on the big screen.

All of this because I didn't answer the phone. It seems like the kind of thing Oscar would do, beat my brother to a pulp and then drop him off here as a warning. In fact when I think about it- It's not even the worst that he's done. I try to concentrate on the match happening before me as Bella hands me another one of those cinnamon drinks which I down in one swig. The whistle blows for half time, my heart hammers in my chest, is this it? Is this the big moment? I search the field as the players slow their pace, wandering in different directions towards their drink bottles.

I see that icy head of hair jogging in the opposite direction to me, just as the heavens open and heavy rain falls onto the crowd. There's lots of squeals from girls around us but Bella and I just laugh as we get absolutely soaked through.

"What do we do now? Will the match be cancelled?" I shout to her over the crowd.

"No, they'll put the roof on in a moment." She giggles as she tries to shield her hair from the rain.

"I don't know why I didn't think to bring a coat, it's October for fuck sake."

"Um, Lou..."

I glance at Bella, noticing her eyes are fixed on the field, she gives me a small nod and I follow her line of sight. Grenville is jogging towards me, shirtless. His body glistened deliciously with rain, sweat and mud. I'm mesmerised as his abs ripple with each step. Is it even possible to have that many abs? He has the body of a god- there's no other way to describe such muscle definition. As he gets closer I see he's clutching something black and red in his hands, is that a jacket?

When he reaches me he vaults over the barrier in one swift and impressive movement putting those gorgeous sweat drenched abs right in my line of sight. He unfolds the jacket, and thanks to a subtle elbow to the ribs from Bella, I finally tear my eyes away from a bead of sweat dripping from his body and stand up in front of him. I give my dazed head a shake. If I thought this guy's cologne was intoxicating, I can confirm it has nothing on the scent of him post rugby game.

He drapes the jacket over my shoulders, it's one of those official Grenville Varsity style jackets and it's huge on me. It's warm and it smells like him which makes me forget all of the troubles waiting for me after the game. I'm 100% sure this is the most romantic thing anyones ever done for me.

His eyes flash with something before he leans down and whispers in my ear, "The cameras are on us right now, so smile and act like I've just told you I'm looking forward to bending you over in that library later."

I glance at myself on the big screen behind him just in time to see my complexion redden. He does up the buttons on the jacket and smirks as his fingers graze my nipple, I shudder from the touch.

"Perfect, my name looks good on you," he says with a wink and then vaults back onto the pitch and runs back to join his team mates.

The crowd is gasping, but I'm still frozen and red from his comment. Glancing down at my top, I see it does indeed say "Grenville".

Chapter 12:

The whispers of the other students follow me all the way back up to the main building after the match. An electricity dances in the air due to the magnificent Oxford defeat. I'd never really had Grenville down as a sporty guy, but he moved with the kind of precision and finesse you'd expect a professional to have.

God get a grip of yourself Lou. My stomach fills with the anticipation of his promise to me, *tonight- I'll have some answers.*

Bella is thankfully silent as we walk up the hill, but I can tell she's eager to find out who the mystery man is waiting for me in my room. I didn't stop to speak to Grenville after the game, getting my brother out of here is the priority right now. Especially as I don't know if I'm still picking up the drugs tonight.

When we finally reach my room, I hurl my door open and I'm straight into mother hen mode as I scan the room for my brother. To my relief, I found him lounging shirtless on the sofa with his feet on the coffee table. *Make yourself at home, why don't you?* My relief is washed away with rage as I spot him sitting next to Cora a little too close for comfort. *No way can I allow her to get involved with him.*

I pick up a scatter cushion from the floor and launch it at him.

"Can someone explain who the fuck this is?" Bella drawls as she makes her way to the kitchen, probably after the endless supply of champagne we seem to have.

"Yes Frankie, please enlighten me as to why you're here," I grit through my teeth. Frankie plasters on his cheeky chappy persona, as he gets up from the sofa to grab his shirt.

"I was mugged, I was near here and needed your help. That's all there is to it. But I have to admit, it wasn't the welcome I was expecting from you especially after I did you a favour." He starts pulling out his cigarettes and I smack them out of his hand, sending them to the floor.

"You can't smoke in here you imbecile!" I shout at him.

"Oh, using fancy words now that you're in a fancy place? Just call me a cunt like you usually do." My blood boils and my jaw is tight as I stare him down.

"I think we'll leave you both to it. Lou, see you at the party?" Cora's voice is tentative as she approaches me. I'm too angry to speak so I just nod.

"Nice to meet you Frankie, thanks for the tips." Is that a flirty smile she's giving him? Sweet Jesus... I don't speak to him until the door is closed.

"What are you doing here, Frankie?" I ask calmly, taking in some deep breaths.

"I took a beating to get you out of the meeting tonight. I have the drugs and stashed them somewhere on campus for you to grab."

"Frankie... I..." I start, but he holds up a hand and gives me a tight smile.

"You can't run from the past forever, Lou. He knows where you are and he'll come for you. I'm trying everything I can to keep him occupied but you know as well as I do he won't stop," he warns. "I don't know how much time I've bought you but please do us both a favour and leave the country, just like we planned before. He threatened mum, Lou. He's coming after us all one by one. He would've killed me already but I'm too valuable. The streets don't, and never will, respect his name the way they do ours." He puffs his chest out with pride, I give him a tight smile. He doesn't get enough credit for keeping this from our door for so long.

"I can't leave Frankie, we've been through this. This is why I'm here. I'm here to gain power and influence so that we can cut him off at the root and get Dad out of that hell hole." He pulls me into a tight hug, I close my eyes and savour the sense of home and safety he gives me.

"I don't know how much longer I can stall him, he wants you. Wants to destroy you and everything around you for what you did." He murmurs against my head. I pull away as an idea suddenly comes to life.

"What if I found a way to make us invaluable, and my presence here invaluable to him? I'll sell the drugs he's given us, I can sell it all but I'll need help, I can't shift them by myself. You'll return him the cash first thing in the morning, tell him you need more. Make him see that he can make more money than he ever dreamed of here. But in order to do that we both need to be alive."

It's a bonkers plan even by my standards, but I know it's the best way to buy us more time until I've gained influence. Enough influence to finally free Dad so he can bring Birmingham to heel- more importantly Oscar to heel.

"Have I told you that you're a genius? There's only one thing he loves more than you- power and money. He's desperate to prove himself to the streets." I shiver at his words.

"Pitch it to him smart, Frankie. Show him he can be walking and talking with the Elite if he plays his cards right. He's insecure about his background, the fact he's not from gang royalty- an outsider. Make him think that it's all his idea and he'll do it. I'm sure of it. I'm close to getting the information I need to get Dad out, but I need more time. Can you do this for me?" I rest my hands on his arms and search his brown eyes- the same colour and shape as mine, as our Dad's.

"I'll do it, but only the blonde helps. I don't like the other one, she gives me the ick" he mutters and holds out his hand for me to shake.

"Bella is probably the best person for the job, I choose who works with us. Those are my demands." I stand firm on my choice, I'll need them both to help me and I'm sure I can trust them.

"Done," he mutters with a smirk. I grip his hand firmly and shake it.

"If it doesn't work out here, with that kind of thinking- you could be running Birmingham. She would be good to you." I huff and shake my head at him, the thought of running this small job gives me anxiety as it is. No way could I handle being a mob boss. I'd crack from the pressure after the first week.

"By the way, what tips did you give Cora?" I ask him, changing the subject. He gives me a goofy grin.

"I told her exactly how to land a decent uppercut to that Oxford wanker." His smile grows more. Another worry to add to the list.

Chapter 13:

By the time I make it to the observatory, I'm a sweaty mess. Although I'm grateful Frankie hid the stash well, I wasn't expecting to be trudging through the forest surrounding the Grenville grounds in heels. Thankfully after a quick rundown of what I needed to achieve in one night the girls took the product, no questions asked.

The expensive tote bags full of cocaine dangle from our arms as we walk into the obsidian dome. We head straight for the bar, pushing our way through the sea of sweaty bodies on the dance floor. I let out a breath of relief as I people watched, there wasn't a single person not already drunk so this should be an easy job.

I learned very quickly during my short time as a peddler for Oscar, that the trick is to catch them before the alcohol-high wears off. It's not something I'm proud of, but I was young and stupid and had a persuasive and ambitious boyfriend at the time. At sixteen years old I'd have done anything for Oscar.

Shaking away the thoughts, I neck the Vodka cranberry Bella hands me, she looks at me as if she's seeing me for the first time.

"I think it's best if we split up," I shout to them over the music, but Bella shakes her head.

"No chance in hell, you're too high profile for this shit now. All eyes are on you after today and if you get caught you're fucked! Leave it to me and Cora, we'll get rid of it somehow." I shake my head at her.

"There's absolutely no way I'm going to let you both take the fall for this if we get caught!" I shout back.

"This is my mess that I have to clean up." With some hesitancy, they nod, clearly coming to the conclusion that my stubbornness won't be beaten today.

"I'll be careful, this isn't my first Rodeo. Meet me back here in two hours, we can regroup then." They both take their orders without complaint and go their separate ways. I watch as Cora heads over to where the Oxford boys are dancing, she blends in seamlessly, and like rabid dogs in heat they swarm her.

Turning, I see Bella head into the girls bathroom, smart move. Drunk crying girls are always some of the best customers. I look around, picking my first target carefully while I run through every possible scenario in my head. I have to paint the picture of innocence, just a stupid drunk girl who bought way too many drugs and wants some people to party with. Just as I think I've found my first victim, a tall gaunt looking boy with a sallow face and long dark hair, I spot Sebastian walking to a red door I hadn't noticed as we came in. He looks around, to see if anyone is watching and heads inside. *How curious.* I saunter over to the door slowly, my hand rests on the cold silver handle when I reach it. What could be behind it? Why did he look so shifty when he went in? I glance around me to check I've not been spotted either, as I turn the knob and push the door open.

My senses are assaulted as I step through, the flashing strobe lights make everything move in slow motion so I place my hand on the corridor wall to keep the disorientation at bay. I can't hear anything over the music as I walk slowly towards the room, my intuition screaming at me to turn around and go back. I know in the pit of my stomach that whatever is in that room is something that I do not want to see. I swallow down the fear and pick up my pace. As I reach the entrance, the smell hits me. I cover my nose with my sleeve as I take in the scene in front of me.

"What. the. fuck." I mutter. The room is circular, just like the one I came in from. Except instead of their being DJ in the middle of the room, there's chaos.

I only recognise about eight of the men, still in their Grenville rugby kits smashing glasses and flipping tables. Sweat gleams from the naked women in the centre, the men each taking turns to fuck them senseless. I tilt my head to the side trying to figure out how anyone can get their leg over their head like that. Sebastian picks up a bottle of champagne and pours it over the woman's body, taking his time to lick her clean afterwards. My eyes flick to the waiter who's standing with his back pressed firmly to the wall, holding a silver tray full of hors d'oeuvres. One of the guys I recognise as Thomas Crawley, flips the tray out of the waiter's hands. The food splatters to the floor as he bursts into laughter.

Before I know it, hands grab at me from all directions pulling me away from the safety of the exit.

"Calm it down." Sebastian's voice hisses in my ear. I struggle against him as he drags me towards the middle of the room. I'm thrown to the floor like a doll and as I lift my head, I find myself surrounded by twelve lustful men.

"I thought the main entertainment wasn't until later." Thomas says as he licks his lips. Terror spreads through me as he undresses me with his eyes.

I glance around, trying to find an escape but they've got me surrounded.

"You know, it's always thrilling when the hounds don't have to hunt for the fox. I was willing to put in the time and effort into winning your hand, but I think I'll just take it instead." Sebastian lunges for me and my body snaps into fight mode. But before I can kick him in the balls, he's dragged backwards and sent flying into the wall where the waiter still stands.

"Tsk, Tsk. Have you no respect, Sebastian?" Grenville says, his eyes filled with blazing fury. I breathe a sigh of relief as his eyes meet mine.

"Are you all stupid enough to touch what is mine?" He drawls, in that signature bored tone of his. The men shake their heads and avoid his gaze. I don't blame them, Grenville commands the room without even trying.

"Are you alright?" He asks as he holds out a hand for me, I take it and nod ignoring how shaky my legs are. He looks me up and down, assessing the damage.

"Now as for that evening entertainment you're so desperate for..." He says as he unbuttons the cuffs on his white shirt. He rolls up his sleeves slowly, I watch as the men around us back away. Grenville saunters over to where Sebastian is lying on the floor, he grabs him by the throat and lifts him into the air like he weighs nothing.

I don't look away as he beats him to a pulp, blood hits the walls, Jackson Pollock style and speckles his crisp white shirt. His usual swept back hair falls over his face as he lands punch after punch on Sebastian's face. His eyes roll as his head droops and finally, Grenville lets go. His body hits the floor in a crumpled heap.

Chapter 14

I clutch my bag to my chest like a shield, as Grenville escorts me back out to the party, his arm wraps around my waist to keep me steady as my legs shake with every step. We stop briefly at the bar, as he grabs two neat whiskeys. He knocks his back and gestures for me to do the same. I'm surprised nobody in here has made a comment on his bloody shirt, then again, would anyone dare?

"I didn't think you were the squeamish type." He says as the whiskey burns the back of my throat.

"I thought you had seen worse than that, where you come from." I roll my eyes at him, so we're back to this now are we?

"Blood- I can manage. Beatings? Easy peasy. But almost being raped was not on my bingo card for today, my apologies if I seem a little rattled." I neck the last of the liquid and I feel the muscles in my body start to relax.

"Come outside with me, the fresh air will help." He surprises me as he entwines his hand with mine, I look down and my gaze snags on the blood drying on his hands.

"Don't you want to wash that off?" I ask, cocking an eyebrow at him. He smirks as he begins to lead us towards the door, all eyes are on us as the crowd parts like the red sea for him.

"No, let Sebastian's blood serve as a warning to everyone else here."

Why does that make me feel all warm and fuzzy inside? Once we were out of the dome, I gulped down the fresh air, savouring the stinging sensation it gives my lungs. We walked with our hands still joined, over towards a bench a little way from the Observatory. With the stars twinkling down on us, this could almost be considered as romantic. Grenville sits down and looks up to the sky, he pulls out an old fashioned silver lighter in the shape of a snake and a packet of cigarettes.

"What were you doing in there?" He asks calmly as he lights it. I panic, trying to figure out a way to lie my way out of this. I couldn't tell him I'd gone in there with a bag full of Coke with the intention to sell it. He turns to look at me, his silver eyes narrow like I'm a puzzle he's desperate to solve.

"I could ask you the same thing." I say boldly as I try to buy myself time to think of a good enough lie. He says nothing, shifting us into an uncomfortable silence. I decided to change the subject, anything to keep the questions coming back around to me. *God I'd be terrible in a police investigation.*

"You know, you shouldn't smoke. It's bad for your health." He lets out a small laugh, my attempt at changing the subject goes down like a lead balloon.

"I'm not an idiot, you know. You and the bimbo twins are less than... discreet."

I watch as his tongue rolls over the inside of his cheek.

"What is it you think I was doing exactly?" Had he been watching me this entire time? Did he follow me into that room?

"Selling Class A drugs is a criminal offence. You'd be sent to worse places than Birmingham for that." My stomach plummets, *shit*. How do I get out of this one?

"What can I say? I'm a poor girl who's got to make a living somehow." I turn away and stare straight ahead, staring at the shadows of the trees of the surrounding forest.

"If we're going to continue our little charade, it has to stop. I can provide what you need so give me what you have left and I'll be sure it's destroyed."

"Charade? What Charade is that exactly?" I cross my arms and narrow my eyes.

He doesn't answer, or look at me. He holds out his hand for my bag.

"You have the look of a startled animal at the moment, which tells me there's more to this than simply making money."

Shit, shit, shit!

"No more games Garrick, be honest with me. Why are you here selling drugs at *my* university."

I suck my bottom lip between my teeth, as I try to figure a way out of this. I can't give him the truth or hand over the drugs. I need to make us indispensable to Oscar, I can't do that if I don't have anything for Frankie to throw at his feet. Then one by one he will pick us off like flies caught in a spider's web.

"I'm sorry but I'm not divulging my justifications to you. You've been awful to me since the moment we've met, for absolutely no reason at all. Trust is earned, Grenville."

He looks me up and down in a bitter assessment and runs his tongue over his teeth, the last of my self control snaps.

"Why did you even bother to save me?" I shout as I clutch the handle of the bag tighter. He throws his head back in malicious laughter.

"Save you? Oh no, I'm not some knight in shining armour I assure you. My motivations are entirely selfish. I can't be seen courting damaged goods, could I?"

Tears fall of their own admission, how could I have been so stupid? I let Bella and Cora fill my head with fantastical ideas of him actually liking me. When in reality, he just wants to use me for his own selfish reasons. Well I won't be used. I clutch the bag tighter, my mind made up. My heartbeat pounds in my ears as I slowly take my feet from my heels. I keep eye contact as I lean closer to him.

"You really are an entitled cunt, you know that?" I snarl, my accent thick and adrenaline coursing through me like a bolt of lightning. My stomach twists as I feel the leather bag in my hand press hard against my skin, had it been a knife I'd be bleeding out. I don't wait around for his next sarcastic comment, I bolt from the bench running so fast my lungs sting. I aim for the trees down the hill. Not daring to look back, I focus my breathing just like Frankie taught me. Breathing is in my control and if I keep breathing no matter how shit I feel I'll be able to keep running. I stumble on a rock, hidden in the shadows half way down as the incline increases. My body flies down to the ground. The pain doesn't register thanks to the adrenaline and I hear his footsteps coming down the hill after me, loud and thunderous in the silence. I push myself to keep the momentum going, knowing that if I don't the pain will sear through me.

When the incline stops, I scramble up from the floor and keep going, tears and mud no doubt staining my face. As I get closer to the tree line, someone else emerges from it. My eyes grow wide as the shadowy figure comes into the moonlight, I come to a halt, realising I'm cornered by the two men I desperately want to get away from.

He's found me. Oscar is here.

Chapter 15:

Oscar steps out from the shadows, with his usual confident swagger. The dark blue chequered shirt rolled up at the sleeves revealing his tattoos. A shiver runs down my spine as I stare at the Virgin Mary on his forearm, the one he'd got for me.

His white teeth gleam in the moonlight as he rubs his hands together like he's won a prize. Licking his lips, he leans to the side as he assesses me, the action bringing up all of those memories I've so carefully locked away.

"How are you, Louisa?" His low gravelly voice makes me want to vomit.

"I have to say, when I found out where Frankie was hiding you I was shocked." He places his hand over his chest and starts to move towards me, I back up a couple of steps in reaction.

"Still a flighty little thing I see. Are you having fun playing dress up?"

I shake my head, refusing to believe this is happening, *Frankie told me the meeting was off, that he'd sorted it so he'd be at arm's length.*

"There you are," comes a voice from behind me. "Everyone's looking for you, we should head back inside. Oh, who's this?" Despite his comments just now, his hand is a welcome comfort as it grazes my waist. It keeps me grounded, here in the present, not stuck in my own nightmares from the past.

"Oscar," he answers himself, moving towards us with his hand outstretched. "I'm one of Louisa's old friends."

His grin is sadistic, I can tell he's sizing Grenville up. I also know what's in his pocket and I need to get Grenville away from here now, the last thing I need is explaining how the heir to the university was stabbed to death.

"Oscar Carr? Isn't it?"

I freeze. *How the fuck does he know about Oscar?*

"That's right." He narrows his eyes at Grenville.

"Well, this is private property, I don't mean to be rude but we have quite strict rules here." Grenville is being polite enough, but I know Oscar and how he thinks- he's probably ready to shank him for being too nice.

"I don't see any Police or security around. It was pretty easy to get in. Now if you don't mind, I was having a private conversation, so run back up the hill to your fancy party while I catch up with my old friend."

Oscar takes a step towards me, his arm outstretched like he's about to grab me. my instincts kick in as I land a punch square in his face.

"You will not ever touch me again. You'll get your money, I'll send it back with Frankie tomorrow," Grenville's hand tightens around me. He laughs as he wipes the blood from his lip onto with his thumb.

"I'm here to collect now. I've been watching you all day- you've only been in there selling for what? An hour max? Not enough to get rid of all those drugs I gave your brother, I can't trust him to get anything done when it comes to you. So I thought I'd swing by and see to it that he does."

Panic ripples through me, if he'd been here all day watching me, then he knows that the girls have the other bags...

"I have your money, but as Miss Garrick said- it was due to leave tomorrow with her brother." Grenville's voice has an edge to it as he steps in front of me- putting himself between me and Oscar.

"Go and get it then. Leave Lou here and get my money." He whispers as he squares up to Grenville, why isn't he afraid of Oscar? If he knew who he was, then surely he'd know what he's capable of. The guy is running the streets right now, his name is in everyone's mouth. It wouldn't take much digging to find out how he got his hands on the Birmingham throne.

"You see the building up there? My name is on the front. I made sure to put it in big bold letters, so that even a disgusting illiterate cunt like you could read it if you really tried. I also own the ground you're standing on, I own everything here in fact. Now be a good little errand boy, and crawl back under whatever rock you crawled out from."

I close my eyes, bracing myself for Oscar's fury. His insecurities stem from his background and for someone to treat him like this, like he's nothing? God help us all.

I open them again, realising that it's gone eerily quiet, just in time to see Oscar pull his knife. I yank Grenville backwards, away from the glinting silver.

I watch helplessly as Oscar lunges at Grenville. I could run, but after what he just did for me? I'd be a dick. It's like watching a dance, but one of them is clearly more seasoned than the other... Every time Oscar lunges, he dodges it effortlessly. Grenvilles fist collides with the underside of Oscar's jaw, sending him flying to the floor. He lies there for a moment, dazed and then starts holding his chin and wailing. A wave of satisfaction floods me, he's never looked more pathetic.

"That is a shattered jaw for you, intense pain that never fully goes away even if it does heal."

I glance at Grenville who's examining his hand as if he's got a bit of dirt on it, that's when I spot the large silver ring on his middle finger.

"You'll want to get yourself to A&E quickly if you want it fixed, I assume you don't have a private doctor that'll see to you. God the wait times in there are appalling at the moment, certainly wouldn't catch me waiting around for hours in there." He crouches down next to Oscar as he continues to wail. "You'll have your money when Mr Garrick sees fit to deliver it, then afterwards I suggest you seek some other family to torment. There are bigger and badder people in this world than you, you don't want to make an enemy of me- my resources, unlike yours, are limitless."

The edges of my vision begin to blur as a sense of relief washes over me, I stumble on the spot, my body suddenly feeling like it's floating. I feel his warm hands wrap themselves around me, holding me steady again. My breathing picks up as I feel a cold sheen of sweat forming on my forehead, I lean into his hard muscular body.

"What's happening?" I manage to mutter, as I'm lifted into the air.

Chapter 16:

When I open my eyes, the lights in my normally dimly lit bedroom seem too bright. Blinking rapidly, I try to adjust to it. The voices in the room with me seem far away, I try to call out but my mouth is too dry. The bed dips as someone sits next to me.

"Easy now, Lou," I recognise Frankie's voice and feel nothing but relief. *He's alive. Oscar didn't get to him.*

"What the fuck happened?" I managed to croak out, "Your boyfriend managed to fight off the biggest baddest mother fucker in Birmingham- that's what happened." Frankie says giddily as his face slowly comes back into focus.

"What happened after that I mean?" I say, wincing at the sharp pain in my head.

"You went into shock. Then once Oscar got his head kicked in by Ben- who's my new favourite person by the way- he carried you back up here and sent for a fancy arse doctor to check you over. You've not been out long, only eight hours." He presses a kiss to my forehead then turns to my bedside table, grabbing me a glass of water.

I wince again as I try to sit up. Frankie holds the glass up to my lips, I gulp down the cool liquid greedily.

"Is Grenville okay?" I ask as my throat springs back to life from the cool water.

"Perfectly fine, Garrick." the hairs on my arm stand to attention. *I only know one person that gets that kind of reaction out of me.*

"I'll give you two some privacy," Frankie says as he gets off the bed and heads out the room. I turn to look at him sheepishly. He's sat in the plush armchair by the window, his face slightly cast in shadow as the light pools in around his silhouette. My stomach drops as I notice his ripped shirt that's stained with blood, was he hurt? Has he been here all night? Then I remember what Frankie had said, he'd *carried* me up here- while being injured himself by the looks of it. My eyes landed on his unreadable face, my mind reeling with questions. The cool air from the open window kisses my skin as I sit up in bed, I glance down at myself. Why am I in a silvery silk night dress? I grab the sheets back up to cover myself, did he get me changed?

"Don't panic, Cora and Bella changed you. I didn't touch you." His tone is cold and drips with venom, what a confusing enemy he is. At least with Oscar I understand his motivations for making my life as difficult as possible, but Grenville? It's like playing a game of chess blindfolded. *Infuriating.*

"Why did they do that?" My cheeks heat, already knowing what wicked game those girls' are playing. I curse them silently.

"They wanted to make sure you weren't unseemly as I refused to leave your side." My brows furrow, "Yes, I was here all night. I wanted to have that little conversation of ours before you had the chance to run off again." His eyes flash with anger and my stomach twists as the memories from the night before come flooding back. The room with the red door, the way my bones had chilled when Oscar had stepped out from the shadows. I hiss from the pain in my head.

"You have a lot to process, but I won't allow you any more pain medication until you've eaten. I'm going to get your breakfast and while you eat I'll talk. If you choose to run after I've explained everything..." he runs his tongue over his teeth as he leans forwards, "let's just say there isn't a single place on this earth that you could run to, where I wouldn't find you." I inhale sharply at his threat, after seeing what he is capable of last night- I don't doubt that for a second.

"I'm not hungry, I just want to sleep and for you to leave." I try to give him all the sass I can muster but my damn stomach betrays me and lets out an embarrassing growl. He flashes me a smile that I'm sure would bring girls to their knees. I watch intently as he gets up and leaves the room. I hear pots and pans clattering around, *what the hell is he doing in there?* Grenville was quite literally born with a silver spoon in his mouth, theres no fucking way he knows how to make breakfast, if he did, I doubt it would be edible.

As I try to relax, the shock of the night catches up to me. The gut-retching feeling of having twelve men circle me, all of that adrenaline I'd felt when running from him, seeing Oscar for the first time in years, watching Grenville break his jaw with little effort. He had been like a knight in shining armour, last night. The kind of thing a girl dreams of when they're sixteen… I had never been a damsel in distress and I'm not sure I liked the feeling of being one.

I had always been the strong one in our family, especially after my Dad took the fall for my mistakes. Guilt had forced me to take on that family responsibility. I had cared for Mum, her disposition so delicate without my Dad around, kept Frankie out of trouble the best I could. Tried to get us all out of that hell hole. But now? This situation feels like a whole different ball game, I can't shake the feeling that I have landed myself in an even bigger mess than before. Oscar is probably off licking his wounds right now but there's not a doubt in my mind that he'll get me back for this. He'll find a way to punish me, I may be smart when it comes to Academia, but battle strategy is not my forte. I haven't seen the last of him.

I let myself wallow for just a second, before wiping away the tears that have fallen. I take a deep breath as the kitchen falls silent, the anticipation builds in my stomach. What does someone like him, a man who owns everything, want with me?

The door opens slowly and Grenville walks in holding an ornate silver tray, he smiles at me as he sees how taken aback I look. The gesture seems so… human. He places the tray down gently on the bed and I gaze down at the meal in front of me.

"Did you make this?" I ask and I can't help but smile a little as I look at how perfectly sliced the strawberries look next to the fluffy pancakes that are just the right shade of brown.

"I'm not totally useless, Garrick," he says as he cocks an eyebrow at me and smirks. He runs a hand through his hair, pushing back the strands that have come down over his face and I realise he's changed. The bloody shirt has been replaced with a black T-shirt and... sweet lord are those grey joggers? I avert my eyes back to the breakfast and make a little coughing noise to clear my throat.

"You eat, I'll talk. Questions after." The softness he had a moment ago disappears as quickly as it came. I nod and sit up further, hunching my back over slightly as I pick up a strawberry and take a bite. He watches every single movement my mouth makes and I try not shrink away from the piercing silver eyes.

"The conversation you overheard in the library, between me and my father, he had just finished telling me that I was to be married by the end of next year. A woman I didn't choose but a woman worthy of the Grenville name."

My heart sinks, of course someone like him has an arranged marriage.

"I've always wanted to break tradition, despite my upbringing I've always had an unrealistic view of marriage. I've spent most of my life disobeying my fathers orders and rebelling at every chance I got. I didn't attend Grenville when I was supposed to, I decided to go travelling for 3 years because I knew once I was here it would be the beginning of the end of my free will. I spent three years living under a different name, savouring the anonymity and thanks to my mother, I was left to my own devices. That is until he found me. I had no intention of coming back of course, but then I discovered his secret." I raise an eyebrow at him as I take a bite of the pancakes, desperate to absorb every piece of information he gives me. "My father has cancer, the type that's incurable. I suppose there's still some things in life that money cannot buy."

I give him a sympathetic look, but stay silent.

"Anyway, I decided it was time to face the music so I came back. Mainly for my siblings sakes, and my mothers of course. Since then, the pressure has been far greater than I anticipated, my father's outburst in the Library was supposed to be completely private and I do apologise for my actions that followed. When you fell from the window, in that ghastly manner, I knew right there and then that you were my saviour in disguise. A woman who dared to defy me would be the perfect candidate for pissing my father off to no end. Your background just made it that bit more perfect."

My cheeks heat again and I feel so inadequate, this entire thing was just to piss his Dad off? How could I have been so stupid?

"I used you so that my father would break off the engagement, I knew her family would want to keep her reputation protected and be less than pleased if there were rumours of me shagging some girl from Birmingham. But her family has been persistent, so has my father. They are determined to paint this as me lashing out due to his diagnosis, my actions caused by grief. So I propose that we continue this little charade for a little while longer, until the engagement is off and then you are free to do as you please." There's no softness in his eyes, no remorse for what he's put me through since coming here. Bella and Cora couldn't have been more wrong about his motivations. *I've replaced a demon for the devil.*

If Professor Daphne were here she'd convince me to go through with it all, but if he's not interested in me in the slightest how am I supposed to influence his political decisions? I'm well aware of the powers women hold over men but I'm fairly certain that I have absolutely none in this situation. *I guess there's only one way to find out.*

I don't try to hide my body from him as I get up and walk towards the chair. His gaze never leaves mine, but I don't miss the flicker of heat in his eyes.

"What's in it for me?" I ask coldly, leaning in close. I'm Louisa fucking Garrick, Mafia royalty, the person who gained entry into this school despite her background.

His lips twitch, "I thought you'd never ask. While you were out cold I did some more digging into your past, Frankie was also more than kind enough to provide me adequate information on your upbringing. How does enough money to get yourself and your family out of Birmingham sound? If that's not enough I can give you a job for life at any company I own, a weekly allowance from my personal funds while this arrangement continues, your own private staff... Everything a girl like you could dream of. All you have to do is say yes."

"There's something else I want," I say as seductively as I can, call me petty, but I'm not afraid to use every trick up my sleeve to get what I want.

"Anything," he says in barely a whisper, his eyes breaking away from mine for the first time as he stares at my lips.

"You said last night that your reach is limitless. Prove it."

He looks me in the eyes again, the tension between us is intoxicating and I savour every moment even though I am walking a very dangerous line.

"Name it." He licks his lips and moves closer.

"My father's in prison, I want him out. All the charges dropped."

His brows furrow slightly, perhaps he'd not researched me as well as I thought he had. "You'd do all of this, for your family?" he asks, moving to stand up, breaking the tension like a hot knife through the skin.

"I have done worse for them." I mutter as I gaze out of the window, the memories making the pounding in my head intensify.

"Consider it done, until next week then, Garrick. I have a dinner to attend Wednesday evening in London, you *will* accompany me. I'll have clothes sent here." *London?*

"I can't next week, I have tests to prepare for," I mutter as my packed calendar zooms through my head.

"Someone else can take it for you if you wish." *This entitled, fucking prick!*

"I'm not cheating, Grenville. You do know some of us have a fucking work ethic."

"I'm glad to hear it, Garrick, you'll have no problems studying the backgrounds of my dinner guests next week then." He flashes me the smuggest grin that I'd take immense pleasure in wiping off before he leaves me alone in my room, wondering what the hell I've just agreed to.

Chapter 17:

I spend the next week doing my lessons virtually from my room after Grenville insisted to everyone that I must have an unnecessary week off before this dinner.

Professor Daphne has been visiting every evening to instruct me on the correct etiquette of seducing the richest man on the planet. I don't bother telling her that her efforts are in vain, I'll admit the tension between us is like an insatiable itch that needs to be scratched, but there's no way in hell Grenville will fall for silly parlour tricks. Nonetheless, I play along as best I can. All this flipping hair, sipping tea and fake laughing is exhausting. Each time she finally leaves I savour the feeling of my facial muscles relaxing. Then there's the upkeep, my days, despite being put on "bed rest," are filled with people preening and pawing me. I was waxed from head-to-toe on Wednesday, nails trimmed and painted with some kind of non-chip polish -which took a lot longer than I expected- on Thursday. I'd drawn the line at cutting my ebony hair off into a sleek bob. By Friday, I barely recognise myself. Do I look beautifully polished? Yes. Do I feel like myself? No. I feel like I'm Grenville's living doll. All of this stuff was numbing my brain, I almost squealed when Professor Daphne brought in an enormous white board on wheels with names of all the dinner guests and their jobs written neatly across it. Now this is me, no illusion or magic make-up, just plain old words there for the taking. Knowledge is my kind of power.

Professor Daphne has circled the ones in her rival political party, I take notes and hang on her every word. Once she's left, I load up my laptop and start scouring the internet vicariously for some sort of scandal that they might be linked to but to my disappointment, I come up cold every time. How can there be no trace of any of their mistakes on the internet?

Bella and Cora have been in their element sparing no expense when Grenville's black card arrives. I'd felt bad about it until they remind me in a passing comment that I may as well take what I can get just to see if he is as "Limitless" as he says. So I start joining in with the online shopping, relishing at the thought of all the notifications he'll receive. I imagine him pinching the bridge of his nose each time his stupid fancy watch alerts him of a new transaction, the thought brings me nothing but joy.

On Sunday night, Bella cracks open a bottle of champagne and fills me and Cora in on the latest gossip. I listen intently, totally enthralled in the lives of the rich and famous, as we drink and giggle until our stomachs growl. Pulling out my phone, I order us Pizza then run to my room and pull on my favourite light grey loungewear set. The leggings are tight but the T-shirt flares out enough over my stomach that I will be able to hide my bloated pizza belly later. Grabbing one of my fluffy blankets from the end of the bed, I walk back into the living room and can't help but smile when I see them both cackling at each other with a pink clay mud mask on. It's the first time since coming here that I feel any resemblance of normality, I didn't really have female friends back in Birmingham and the ones I did get close enough to were always just trying to get in with Frankie.

"Lou, your phone has not stopped dinging," Bella calls from the sofa when she sees me come in.

I launch myself down into the comfy cushions and wrap the blanket around me. Bella grabs my phone and starts howling with laughter before passing it to me. My eyes grow wide as I look at the notifications, all 57 of them from Grenville, or "Dick Head" as he's named in my phone.

"Why the fuck have you bought a £15,000 watch from Cartier?!"
"Answer the fucking question."
"£70 on takeaway?!"

They're all pretty much the same and I grin down at them.

"Are you going to answer?" Cora asks, her eyes gleaming through the pink decorating her face.

"No, I'm going to leave him on read," I say smugly as I put my phone on silent and place it face down next to me. Thankfully before we can get into it anymore, the pizza arrives with an aggressive knock.

"Jesus," Bella says, as she goes over to the door.

"Oh shit."

I turn to see what's wrong, and my stomach drops. In he strolls. Ruining my perfectly normal night by gracing me with his presence. I notice he's still in his dark grey suit, despite it being late.

"What are you doing here? Our arrangement doesn't start until next week, so go and bore someone else with your pretty little speeches."

Bella and Cora exchange a look and both take a swift exit into Cora's room, leaving me to fend for myself.

"£150,000 is how much you've spent in a week," he growls after Cora's door closes.

Shit, I didn't think we'd spent that much.

"Well... I... needed new things," I say matter of factly.

"£150,000 worth of new things?" He crosses the room in a few slow strides, his hands in his pockets.

"Yes, £150,000 worth of things. You want me to look and dress the same as everyone else in this fucking place then I need new everything. I didn't think it was appropriate for Grenville's girlfriend to wear Primark seven days a week!" I shout back.

"You are an infuriating woman." His face is almost touching mine, right now I don't know if he's going to punch me in the face or kiss me.

"Good, that's the aim. If I'm to be your walking talking living doll for the next few months I should at least have some control because you give me no pleasure at all in this arrangement other than me making your life miserable!"

His eyes flicker with something, and I realise a little too late that I should've chosen my words more carefully. "Pleasure?" he says, his eyes flicking down to my lips.

I freeze, my body replacing my rage with something different. I make the mistake of breaking eye contact and looking at his lips, causing him to smile like he's won.

"Would you like me to amend that for you?" He runs a finger across my exposed collar bone, thanks to my T-shirt going slanted during our argument.

I shiver under his touch, is this real? Would he? He wouldn't, right?

My heart pounds in my chest. This is dangerous territory right now. Did I enjoy the last time he kissed me? Yes. Do I want him to do it again? Yes. But should I allow this line to be blurred? I'd be allowing myself to be an open target for heartbreak when this is all over, I understand that I'm just a means to an end to him. Would it hurt if I reaped *all* of the benefits this sordid arrangement has to offer?

"Watching you battle with yourself is highly entertaining. Perhaps I should do this more often if that's the effect I have on you."

I feel his lips brush mine as he speaks and I can't control my breathing now.

"You are deluded if you think you have any kind of effect on me," I say with as much defiance as I can.

"Hmm, lying is not your strong point, Garrick."

His deep lustrous voice is like a siren's call to my body as heat floods me. His lips meet mine in an unmistakable act of dominance, his tongue is unrelenting as he explores every inch of my mouth. I wrap my arms around the back of his neck and grip the back of his hair as he lifts me effortlessly by my thighs to wrap my legs around him. I savour the moment and think about nothing but him and how his hands feel on my thighs. A weight I hadn't known I'd been carrying lifts from me as I lose myself in him.

He walks towards my room and kicks the secret door open. I break away from the heated kiss in a fury wondering how he'd managed to send the heavy wood flying from the hinges. "I'll buy you a new one," he huffs before launching me down onto the bed like I weigh nothing at all. I squeal as the movement catches me off guard, the noise only seems to egg him on more. He stalks towards me, his eyes darkening.

Reality washes over me like a cold bucket of water, as much as I want this, I can't give into him now.

I move away from him up towards the top of the bed and he crawls towards me like a lion hunting his prey. "Stop." I say as I put my bare foot flat against his chest. He does as he's told and the words are out of my mouth before I can contemplate what I'm saying,

"Good boy." He smirks as he grabs my feet and starts kissing his way up my legs. I shudder from the way his soft lips feel against my skin. I fight back the moan threatening to escape my lips.

"We are not playing by your rules, Garrick."

"No," I breathe out, holding his gaze.

"You defy me yet again? Don't pretend that this isn't exactly what you want." He stays perfectly still as he talks, he's not an idiot and can see how much I want this, but iI don't want to give in to him unless it means he's mine, truly mine.

"I don't play by anyone's rules but my own," he growls and all of Daphne's lessons come swimming to the surface.

"Fine, if you act like a dog then I'll treat you like one. I'll make it a priority to buy you a diamond collar to wear in my presence, I'm sure Tiffany's would be grateful for the design opportunity."

He cocks an arrogant brow as he crawls back off the bed. I breathe a sigh of relief from the distance between us.

"I always get what I want, Garrick, one way or another you'll be begging me to fulfil your every fantasy- and believe me I'm more than happy to oblige." I keep my cool despite the unrelenting need for him flooding through me, I glance down at the door laying on the floor.

"Don't forget to replace that. I want it done by tomorrow. Or you can forget the image of my mouth around your cock." I put emphasis on the 'K' and lick my lips on purpose. I'm more than satisfied with myself as he watches the movement.

He storms out without saying another word, when I hear the front door shut I throw myself back into my cushions, trying to slow the speed of my thoughts down. Cora and Bella squeal as they come bounding into my room.

"Louisa Garrick, I believe you just denied the richest and most powerful man in this university," Cora says as she jumps on the bed. I cover my face with my arm in embarrassment and let out a laugh.

"I don't know what the hell that was, Lou, but if you keep him on his toes like that then you'll have him wrapped around your finger in no time," Bella says with a chuckle. I can hardly imagine what that would be like, but I don't deny that I want it.

Chapter 18:

I don't see him again until Wednesday, the day of the fancy dinner in London. A dinner which I'm confident I'm fully prepared for, when it comes to things like "Proper Conversation" and etiquette. I've thrown myself into the Debutant lessons, thanks to the promise of releasing my Dad from prison hanging in the balance. Despite my attempts to prove myself, the subtle whispers still follow me down the dimly lit prestigious halls. A trip away from the snake pit is exactly what I need. Even though I haven't seen him, his gaze follows me everywhere, thanks to the creepy portraits and marble statues dotted around the halls. The Grenville signature is unmistakable with the light blond hair and silver eyes, as far as I'm aware there are only ever silver haired Grenvilles. I purposefully ignore their silent judgement as I pass now.

I sit on the edge of the couch after Cora leaves for her lectures. My leg bounces up and down involuntarily as I stare at the brand new silver suitcase sitting next to me- I'm all too aware of the running theme here... The silver bow he wrapped my burner phone in, the silver wing that he resides in and now this. My brain can't help but notice these little touches. It makes me feel as if I'm piecing parts of him together- the never ending puzzle that is Benjamin Grenville. I doubt I'll ever know this man body and soul. Well, maybe body if last week was anything to go by.

Despite expecting the knock at the door, it still startles me. I leap from my seat and smooth my carefully curated two piece down as I approach the door. I try to hide my disappointment as I open the door and come face to face with who I can only assume is the driver who has come to collect me.

"I'm here to carry your suitcase and escort you to the car, Miss Garrick," he says, staring straight at the back wall, which is a little odd. I smile and thank him politely as I step aside to let him pass.

"Will Mr Grenville be joining us?" I ask a little too eagerly.

"No, Mr Grenville arrived in London last night, he will be meeting you at the hotel."

Hotel? Now my stomach twists with a different kind of nerves. Will we be in the same room? Or has he booked separate?

Following the driver out without another word, my heels click loudly against the stone. All that time trying to make sure I looked perfect was for nothing. I could've had an extra hour in bed if he'd just told me he wasn't coming. Then again, he always does like to torment me. I haven't heard from him at all since Sunday, did I upset him? *Oh god I've fucked it. He's avoiding me because I was a total arse hole!*

I go back and forth with myself until we reach the car outside, I squint a little at the November sun thanks to how dark the halls of Grenville are. The driver opens the door for me and I slide myself with practised grace into the back of the car. It's about a two hour drive from here to central London and I waste no time pulling out my new wireless earphones from the bag that Bella gifted me. It matches my black and white houndstooth two piece, perfectly. Even if it didn't I probably would've worn it anyway.

The engine of the car is quiet and I feel relief as we pass through the gates, I let my head relax into the heated leather seats.

"I'm sorry but I didn't get your name, I've been in my own head a little bit this morning," I ask the driver, desperate for a distraction of any kind.

"It's Shaw Ma'am."

Okay well that's new... I'm not sure if I like it, surely that term should be reserved for royalty? Am I classed as Royalty now?

"Please, call me Louisa," I say with a smile that doesn't feel like my own. His only response is a smile I catch in the rearview mirror. Guess that conversation is done for the day. I have nothing better to do than gaze out the window, listen to melancholy music and worry about what's in store for me today.

After about an hour, my stomach growls. I'd skipped breakfast earlier because of the anxiety. I wonder how he'll punish me if I'm not there on time. Just like a flick of a switch, Professor Daphne's voice floats through my brain,

"Do what you must to get under that boy's skin. Don't be embarrassing- but show him you're your own woman."

Hmph, sound advice.

"Mr. Shaw, I wonder if we might stop for a bite to eat? I'm practically famished after all this travelling," I ask politely. I clock how he shifts in his seat uncomfortably, so that means we are indeed on a tight schedule.

"Ma'am... Louisa, Mr. Grenville would prefer it if we stayed within the vehicle and travelled to the hotel as swiftly as possible," he says in a well rehearsed manner.

Well I guess he's the one driving, it's not like I can pull over at a fast food place without his permission. I start rummaging through my bag praying that past me thought to pack some sort of snack. But the only thing I can find is a Snickers bar. My favourite chocolate, but far too messy with all this jerking around. I'm not the cleanest eater, even with all the lessons. Sighing in annoyance, I put it back in my bag, "Mother Fucker," I mumble as I take out my phone and begin writing the most un-ladylike message known to man to said Mother Fucker.

"You are the biggest Dick head I've ever come across, how dare you deny me the right to a full stomach."

I hit send but don't close the app, I sit there like an idiot waiting for him to open it.

He Doesn't.

Chapter 19:

As we arrive at the hotel, in the middle of bustling central London, I take a moment to marvel at the beautiful building. It's similar to Grenville in its pale stone exterior but far less gothic. The Inside is just as fabulous, it feels exactly how you'd imagine a palace to feel like, but with modern curves.

After checking in, I head straight up to the penthouse, and I'm greeted by the bright sunlight. The entire front of the room is glass, and is much higher than the other buildings so I have a perfect view of the London Skyline. I rush towards it, pure joy filling me up. I yank out my phone from my bag and take a selfie for the girls. I send it into the group chat we've made to let them know that I've arrived safely and that the driver was not in fact a serial killer. I explore the penthouse thoroughly, heading for the kitchen first, but of course there is no food. *God, doesn't this guy eat?* Unable to stand the hunger pains any longer, I decided to head down to the restaurant after a quick freshen up and a change of outfit. I go with the teal long sleeved jumpsuit that Bella had suggested, paired with some nude heels. God, what I'd give to wear a pair of trainers... I just finish dressing when the lift dings and I scramble up off the bed to see who's arrived.

Again, it's not him. It's a waiter wheeling in a cart full of mouth watering food, the centrepiece being pancakes and strawberries and an obnoxiously large bouquet of white tulips.

"Mr. Grenville sends his apologies."

I give him a small smile and nod, I pull out my phone again and send him a thank you message as I dig into the fresh fruit. He replies almost instantly,

"Wow, gratitude for once."

I roll my eyes and throw it down onto the coffee table.

I TRY AND STILL MY irregular heartbeat as I head down to the restaurant of the hotel. After spending the day cooped up in the room, I'm hoping there's a balcony so I can at least get some fresh air.

I feel hemmed in, in a way that reminds me of a past I'd rather forget. The days I'd spent trapped inside the hotel in Birmingham are a far cry from this, but it also has similarities I can't miss.

I try to push away the thoughts of the day my world got turned upside down and gather myself as I watch the number of floors go down. *You're being ridiculous. Grenville is different from Oscar, I doubt any of this is intentional. How's he to know my triggers anyway?*

The lift doors open to a silent and empty restaurant, I take my first few steps tentatively. Am I the first one here? I feel the long earrings tap the side of my neck as I turn to see where everyone is, a little reminder to be careful not to lose them or else Cora will kill me. I walk past a few of the tables and chairs towards the bar, which is basically a giant mirror. I give myself another quick once over as I approach, I hardly recognise myself. My dark hair is twisted up into a complicated bun of sorts that sits just a little lower than my crown, my face framed with perfectly placed "loose" curls. And I say loose because everything about this is purposeful. The black dress is a total jaw dropper on me. I love everything about it, from the halter neck with a sensual plunging front to the delectably deliberate exposing back that hangs just above my arse.

"Hello?" I call out to the empty bar, I want to sit and rest my feet but I'm not sure how low this dress actually goes whilst seated.

"Well aren't you a pretty little thing." Comes a sneering voice from behind me that I don't recognise.

I whirl around to see a very tall and handsome man holding a glass tumbler filled with amber liquid. My eyes linger on his, familiar and yet not. Silver eyes. Eyes that follow me throughout my day. That's not possible.

"Are you my little brother's side piece from Birmingham then?" His eyes gleam as he unabashedly looks me up and down.

Okay, entirely possible, but his skin is darker than Grenville's and his hair is darker too. Half brothers?

"I suppose I am, are you the other Grenville?" I ask cocking my eyebrow and hip at the same time. He follows the motion without missing a beat as he raises his glass to his lips and takes a sip.

"The bastard, as our father delights in calling me. Has he left you here to fend for yourself?" He gives me a wicked grin that makes me feel like I'm about to be thrown to the wolves. He holds out his arm for me to take and his eyes turn to smoke.

"I see you don't mince your words like your brother insists on doing" I don't hide the flirtation in my voice, he has a very easy and relaxed demeanour about him that has me comfortable taking his arm like he's a familiar friend.

"Mincing words are for important people that have an image to protect, I prefer the Shadows of high society, you'd be surprised how delicious the offers are."

He winks at me and I smile as he leads us to the back of the room towards a door I hadn't noticed before. He stops at the door and offers me his drink, his face full of mischief- sizing me up. I take it and knock it back in one, to my surprise it's whiskey and it burns on the way down.

"Jesus, that's 400 years old," he says, plucking the glass back from my hands and my eyes widen.

"Don't worry, I've got an entire garage full of the stuff. I'll show you some time." He smirks and smoulders again which makes me blush a little.

"Are you ready?" he asks and I nod, taking a deep breath.

He puts his hand on the round doorknob and pauses,

"You scrub up well, by the way," he mutters as he swings it open. My jaw drops, as we walk into the most spectacular ballroom I've ever seen. I thought this was dinner?!

Chapter 20:

I grip his brother's arm tightly, as we navigate our way through the crowd of aristocrats. My palms begin to sweat and my stomach tightens as the conversation around me dies.

"Looks like I'm the luckiest man in here tonight," he whispers in my ear, his warm breath sending shivers down my neck.

"Keep your head up, let's get you a drink." A nod is all I can muster as I search the faces in the crowd for someone I recognise. For him I mean. You'd think that with all of the whispering back at the university, that I'd be used to this treatment by the upper class now. My looks may have changed and I may walk and talk like one of them now, but they can smell an imposter a mile away. I don't think I'd ever be truly exempted by these people. Perhaps that's why I felt unusually comfortable with the stranger on my arm, he enjoys being an outsider, revels in it almost with his 'I dont give a fuck attitude'. I wonder if the sneering still bothers him deep down…

"What's your name?" I ask him discreetly as we continue our slow walk through the crowd.

"Zacharias Grenville, you can call me Zach if you like. I'm not much for formalities," he mutters back as we finally reach the enormous pyramid of champagne glasses. I play it safe and grab one from a tray, these things weren't in my etiquette lessons and I don't think that Zach would appreciate it if I toppled the entire thing over onto him.

"I specifically told you to meet me in the bar," Grenville says through gritted teeth from behind me. I turn to face him, resisting the urge to give him the middle finger.

"Oh look, my baby brother's upset I stole his grand entrance." Zach slaps Grenville's cheek lightly, which he bats away in annoyance.

Zach turns to wink at me, my cheeks turn pink as I give him a smirk and I watch Grenville fidget. I don't think I've ever seen him fidget before. Another crack in the mask... Interesting. Then a wicked idea floats into my mind, like a dark and poisonous Butterfly.

"Would you care to dance Zach? I'm not sure *his* beastly behaviour is appropriate for a lady." I quirk my eyebrow at Grenville and look him up and down, mimicking Bella to the best of my ability.

"Oof, bested yet again brother, I like this one- perhaps we should share her."

Something flashes in his eyes that makes me think that wasn't just a joke.

All eyes are on us as he grabs my waist roughly and pulls me into him, I let out a gasp at the sudden closeness and his intense eyes burn into mine. Zach emanates pure mischief as he throws me effortlessly around the dance floor.

"Whatever it is you're doing with my brother, keep it up. He hasn't been this interesting since his twelfth birthday when he ate so much chocolate cake he was sick." His eyes roam around the room as he speaks; as if he's scouting for danger. I keep my composure calm and will my thoughts to not betray me as I say,

"I don't know what you're talking about." his eyes snap back to mine, curiosity lacing them.

"Despite the blackmail of this arrangement you two have, he feels something when he's with you, he feels like my brother again. Humanity is important to keep hold of when you're handed all the power and corruption in the world." I furrow my brows as I ask tentatively,

"I can understand the pressure he's under, is it your father? Is he... getting worse?".

"The cancer, it seems, has spread to his brain, it's only a matter of time now before Ben makes all the decisions for the entire country." He says quickly, in a perfectly rehearsed manner. I look away from him as I file away the valuable information for later. Looks like Daphne's plan for me will have to start working quicker than anticipated. My heart sinks as I realise this will all be coming to an end sooner than I'd anticipated.

"May I cut in, brother?" The softness in his voice catches me so off guard. that I gasp as I look up at him. There's no sign of that signature Grenville sneer that makes me want to shrivel up and die. Just the perfect gentleman is standing before me now, his hand outstretched towards me. I push away that silly part of me that wishes that all of this was real, that he's utterly smitten with me. I give Zach my well-practised curtsy and take Grenville's hand.

"Of course brother, I have an eternity to get to know your latest play thing." His eyes flash as he smirks before he saunters off back towards the champagne.

I watch him approach the group of middle aged men standing there measuring each other's dicks. They all stiffen slightly as he starts up a conversation in the middle of their war games, he smirks at the balding one and takes a heft swig of his drink.

"Are you done staring at my bastard brother?"

I blink a few times as his hand slides around my waist, gentler than his brother was. His touch leaves a blazing trail on my bare back, I try to ignore it and focus on the steps.

"I thought you said this was a dinner party?" I narrow my eyes slightly at him but his smile never breaks.

"Do me a favour and shut the fuck up so we might get through this torture without me ripping off your head."

"Threatening violence now, Grenville? How proud your mother must be of this fine gentleman you've turned into." I scoff at him, schooling my face into a picture of boredom.

He doesn't reply, just waltzes me around like I'm a China doll.

"Why are you avoiding me?" My insecurities come tumbling out before I can stop them.

"Because you don't deserve my attention. You aren't the centre of my world, Garrick." I look down, hating every inch of him for the effect his icy words have on me. He twirls me around, the sea of faces surrounding us blur together into one as I lose myself in thinking of all the ways I could hurt this man.

How dare he make me feel this way, like I hate myself for not being good enough. I know I'm good enough. I'm better in a lot of ways than his usual type and I know that from the little research I've attempted to do on him. I don't care what he's done for me, all I care about is shoving a knife into him and twisting it, the way he does every single time he looks at me. By the time I'm finished with the House of Grenville it will be a legacy left in shreds. I'll drag every single one of them down with me, not by flirting and wearing fancy dresses, but by doing what I do best- learning.

Chapter 21:

I pay close attention to everyone I'm introduced to, filing away every small bit of information I can gather from the coded conversations I'm privy to. I also notice how much power Grenville commands in the room, there isn't a single person here who's not seeking a moment alone with him, to bend his ear about something they seem to think only he could provide.

The word seems to have spread very quickly about his fathers ill health. They all flock to him, eager to please and hungry for power. The old fat men with receding hairlines gaze at him with nothing but envy and malice in their eyes, but their wives are worse. They all look thin and ghostly, like they're clinging onto their own life force; willing it to give them just a little longer here.

And me? I'm eyed like a piece of meat by everyone. Something here makes my pulse thump and my nervous system scream at me to run. Run away and never come back.

I ignore the hairs standing up on my arms, as we take our seats at the large dinner table. I waltz through the 12 course meal in a delicate and ladylike fashion, I smile when I'm supposed to, laugh when it's needed and pretend to listen intently to their stories of skiing holidays in the French alps. But all the while I plot and puzzle in my anticipation for what will happen when this ends, that is until something makes my ears prick up.

"I hear your blokes lost the seat in the Birmingham constituency yesterday, tough day for the blues dare I say."

I turn my eyes to the man directly opposite me, his voice old and gruff, I smirk as I notice that if he were an animal I'd liken him to a bulldog. *A few more years and he'll be drooling like one too, no doubt.*

A laugh from the end of the table catches my attention and my heart stutters as Zach's eyes flash to mine as he continues sniggering into his whiskey glass.

I look back to the bulldog-esque man and try to sort through the file of images I'd memorised from Professor Daphne's lessons. If I'm correct, his name is Edmund Turnbole, the Earl of Winchester, or is it Viscount?

"Viscount, you know it's not polite to talk politics at the table," Grenville says playfully while cutting into his chocolate cake with his fork.

"Oh come now, you don't think we reds know what you're up to with this girl?" He waves his fork at me as he wraps his fat fingers around his champagne glass.

"No, I don't. Please, enlighten us."

A dangerous tone, memories of a bloodied Sebastian flash in my mind. I sneak a glance down the table as the room falls silent, Zach's no longer in his seat. I shift uncomfortably under the vast sets of eyes on me, it's like the room has sucked in a huge breath, waiting for the explosion to happen.

"I just mean that... well it's a bit coincidental that you lose your foothold in one of the largest cities in the country and suddenly a girl from that very city appears on your arm this evening and a Garrick non the less." He looks me up and down like I'm some disgusting gutter child that's crawled to him begging for money.

"What do you mean by that?" I ask, my cheeks heating as the adrenaline pumps through me, that little feisty creature that has laid dormant scratching at the lid of the box.

Let me play, it sings.

Turnbole stutters a little under my hard gaze and I see Grenville take a big sip of his champagne out the corner of my eye.

"We know all about the Garricks, Birmingham royalty you claim to be. Well not you personally, but your ancestors did. The filthy kings of the underground, thinking they can do as they please whenever they like. Ha! Didn't they get a shock when your father handed himself in after that murder. A messy messy affair. You must have been a child when it happened, so you probably don't remember."

His words trail off as my mind slips away into the memories, I was 16 when it happened. That roiling creature I'd locked away deep inside of me to protect my family, banged against its restraints. The rattling of its chains pulsing through me, *no I will not let this ruin what I've worked so hard to build.*

"... Are you even listening?"

My eyes flash back to his and I rise from my seat, the cool and calm debutant I've been trained to be. "I'm sorry if my being here has offended you, sir. Please allow me to retire to my room so that I cause no further upset." I smile sweetly.

"Louisa, sit down," Grenville says softly to me.

I look at him and the world melts away at the sound of my name on his lips.

"You've offended my date, Viscount," he says, leaning back in his seat.

I watch his knuckles turn white as he speaks, but I realise very quickly it's not that Grenville I should have been watching.

I turn just in time to watch in horror as Zach plunges what looks like a sword straight through the Viscount's back. Blood splatters across his wife and onto me.

I gasp as his eyes bulge from his head.

"Just because you don't think my brother will get his hands dirty, doesn't mean that I won't," Zach smiles as he whispers gleefully in

Viscount's ear. A fountain of blood pools from his mouth and he flops face first into the delicately sliced cake in front of him.

I stare at the body wide eyed, and my breathing picks up. He just...Killed him.

"So sorry for your loss, Dianna. Please, allow me to be the first to congratulate your son on his new position." Grenville grabs his glass and toasts.

"Now, is there anyone else here that would like to comment on my date's ancestral roots?"

He's so calm, not a flicker of anger- total non chalonce. And everyone here is acting like it's nothing?

I look at Dianna who, like me, seems to be transfixed on the pool of blood edging closer to my plate.

"Someone get this cleaned up!" Zach calls out and I look at him, his silver eyes full of life and smugness. "And a bucket for Miss Garrick, I think she's going to vomit on your good China, so make it snappy!".

Chapter 22:

The waiters don't bat an eyelid as they clear away the dead body of the former Viscount. The champagne keeps flowing and the laughter grows louder, my ears ring, hearing nothing but the sound of my own heartbeat. My head is empty, I see and feel nothing inside of it, that creature in the box has been satiated enough that it's curled back up to slumber.

I remember the first time I saw a dead body, my mother had me bundled up in a blanket and held my head to her shoulder as she carried me through our house- singing and tiptoeing as she did. I'd felt sleepy, having been roused from my bed in the dead of night by the flashing blue lights outside our home. I felt the December air nip at my cheeks so I buried my face further into my mother's shoulder. She kept singing.

"Matilda, get yourself over to Barney's. I've let them know you're coming. I've told Bill what's happened, he's furious by the way, so Sergio is going to keep an eye on you until he gets to Barney's. Okay, love?"

I'd lifted my head to see the body of a man laying down in our front garden next to my bicycle, the pink tassels blowing in the wind. I remember thinking that he looked like he could be sleeping. His eyes were wide and looking up to the stars, if there were ever a last thing to look at while being greeted by Death, stars would be my first choice.

"Thanks, Kipper, you're too good to me. I'm sorry about the mess, he caught me by surprise. I'd just turned on the telly to catch up on my soaps when he arrived."

My mum gripped me tighter, her voice soft towards the police man in front of her. He would die soon too.

"Louisa, shall I escort you back to your room?"

Grenville's voice brings me back to the present with a shuddering jolt. I realise that I've been staring at the space the body was.

"Yes, thank you." I force a smile and take his hand as he leads us out of the ballroom and back to the lift.

He says nothing as we step in, I want to say something but my mouth can't seem to form the words. All thoughts of strategy are gone and I feel more exposed than I ever have. I glance at him a few times but he keeps his distance and his eyes fixed on the doors as we travel up to the top of the building. As they open, I step into the room and I'm greeted with my reflection in the windows. I'm still covered in his blood. The dress is ruined by all accounts. My red splattered skin though, that I can't throw away, as much as I want to.

Grenville moves closer to me, watching as I gaze at myself with a blank sickly expression on my face.

"Stay with me," I mutter before I can stop the words coming out of my mouth. Daphne will kill me for being vulnerable with him, for showing any weakness.

"Go and change, I'll fetch you something to drink."

My body moves of its own accord into the bedroom. I grab a pair of silver PJ's out of my suitcase and glance towards the shower. I unclip the dress around my neck and slide it down to the floor, not bothering to pick it up to pack it away. It'll have to go straight in the bin. I take off the heels and take out the earrings, popping them down on the bedside table. I fuss a little with my hair grabbing the pins out impatiently and silently cursing the hairdresser for putting so many in. The tension in my head depletes as my hair tumbles down. I sigh in relief, taking off the perfectly poised mask I wear.

I turn for the shower that's adjoined to the room and stop dead in my tracks as Grenville leans in the doorway. His icy hair is no longer swept back in that perfectly quaft way, it hangs over his forehead almost covering his eyes. His bowtie is undone as well as the top two buttons of his shirt.

    I swallow and walk into the bathroom, not bothering to close it behind me. A silent invitation. I get in and let the hot water flow over me, I don't dare look down at the colour of the water as I scrub at my skin with the soap. The shower door slides open and I don't turn to him, I keep my eyes fixed on the slate grey tiles in front of me.

    He runs a single finger down the side of my neck, down my shoulder and entwines his hand with mine as his chest presses against my back. His body feels like cold hard granite on mine and I sigh with the relief that touch gives me. All thoughts of the evening disappear, suddenly we're the only two people in the world and all that matters is the need I have building up inside me.

    I lean into his body more as he leans down and kisses my neck, the feeling of his lips on my skin ignites a burning inside of me that I didn't know I was capable of feeling. He takes my hand and places it on the shower wall in front of me, the other hand pushes my back- guiding me to bend for him. I do as I'm told. I trust him. A thought I'll probably regret later.

    His hand traces my body and I stand there willing his hand to move to the spot I need him to. To my relief, he does. His fingers rub idle circles around my clit and I moan into the wall, adjusting myself to give him better access, but he doesn't stop. This is all a flex of control I see, to show me he can push me to the edge and drag me straight again. I grind myself against his hand, begging silently for more and he replaces his finger with his thumb, dragging his fingers down the centre of me in one slow excruciating movement. He feels how wet I am, takes his time savouring this new knowledge of the effect he has on me. He moans as he feels me, and pushes two fingers inside- hooking them around that perfect spot.

I wince slightly at the sudden stretch but adjust quickly, giving myself completely over to the pleasure as his thumb rubs me in just the right place. I'm almost bursting but I want more, I want to feel every single inch of this man inside of me and I need it now. I emphasise this by grinding harder on his hand.

"More?" he says and my eyes snap open, the pleasure disappears and replaces itself with cold dread.

That's not Grenvilles voice.

I shove his fingers out of me and whirl around to see a very naked Zach standing in front of me.

"What the fuck?"

My eyes open and I sit bolt upright in the bedroom of the hotel. I look down at my clothes, examining the nightwear I don't remember putting on. I sigh in relief and clasp my clammy forehead, it was just a dream.

Looking out the window, I see it's still dark outside. I don't know where my phone is but I hear low voices coming from the main room. Getting up as quietly as I can from the bed, I tiptoe my way over to the door and press my ear against it, but I can't make out the words. It sounds heated though, should I go out there? Of course I should, this is MY room after all.

Yanking the door open with more force than I care to admit, I find Grenville and Zach looking very tense in their opposite arm chairs. I hesitate for a moment as I remember exactly what these two brothers are capable of.

"What are you doing here?" I say bluntly as I fold my arms.

"You asked me to stay," Grenville says, getting to his feet at once. His face is etched with concern- another confusing part to this ridiculous puzzle.

I glance at Zach but there's nothing written on his face to say he did actually finger me in the shower. He's just drinking his drink, taking in the situation. At least I can relax a little knowing I'd obviously dreamt it, because I would definitely be able to tell by his face if he had, wouldn't I?

"Oh. Yes I remember now," I sigh and touch my head as I feel it starting to throb, too much champagne and gore no doubt.

"Are you okay?" He's next to me in an instant, lifting my chin with his hand, being the sweet caring natured boyfriend I've always wanted.

It makes my blood boil. I slap his hand away from my face and let the rage pour out. "I'm fine, no thanks to you. You drag me here for a dinner party that turns out to be some sort of fucking ball. Then he shows up with his stupid eyes and lulls me into a false sense of security before he literally kills a man in front of me. I am far from alright, those waiters didn't even bat an eyelid as they cleaned up your mess so this is clearly not the first time you two have pulled a stunt like this." Silence follows and I'm suddenly aware that I'm arguing with him in my sleepwear... again.

"I admit, tonight was a mistake. You shouldn't have witnessed that and I apologise, but I do not apologise for my brother's actions. He does what I can't, believe me I wanted to beat the man to death for even so much as thinking about your past, let alone insulting you with it." I want to hit him, I want to ask him why. To ask him to please put me out of my misery and just end this stupid deal.

"I want the truth. For once can you just give me that?" his eyes smoulder the way Zach's do and my knees feel weak at the sight of it. He grips my face in his hands and leans in close.

"You understand power and corruption don't you? The answers are all there in front of you, the truth is whatever I say it is, that's how powerful I am."

I shove his hands from me again and I stalk back into the bedroom and grab the suitcase to start packing my things.

"If you can't even give me the decency of telling me the truth, then you can shove your stupid egotistical deal up your ass and Daphne can shove hers too."

His hands grip my wrists and he spins me around to face him, all traces of concern are replaced with blazing fury.

"What deal did Daphne offer you?" He spits.

"Oh this should be good." Zach mutters sarcastically from the corner.

Oh fuck. How am I supposed to get out of this one?

Chapter 23:

The car is silent as we drive back to Grenville. I give them both the silent treatment the whole drive back. If Grenville has secrets then I will keep mine too, when he'd asked me what I had meant by Daphne's deal, I'd shut my mouth and not opened it since.

I sit in the back of the expensive car with my arms crossed like a petulant child, refusing to answer even the simplest of questions.

I feel like I'm in too deep with these men and this obscene lifestyle that I'm beginning to become accustomed to. But no matter how I feel, I can't back out of the deal with him now. Not when my Dad's sentence rests on my shoulders, I'm sure he would tell me to go deeper if it meant his skin would be saved from rotting in that place.

Zach drives like a fucking maniac, weaving between the traffic like we're in a video game. When we almost crash for the third time in an hour, I finally pipe up,

"Can you please stop driving like that? You're going to kill us all if you're not careful." He throws his head back and lets out a deep husky laugh, why anyone would find it funny I don't know.

"Finally, she speaks. Are you ready to tell me about Daphne yet?" Grenville asks, keeping his eyes on the road ahead. I scowl at the back of his head.

"There is nothing to say, she took me under her wing when I arrived and said she would help me with my debutante lessons if I made sure to pass all my tests, that's it." I've never been the best liar, but clearly my time around Cora has paid off. He seems to buy it, I think.

"I don't believe you," Zach says in a sing-song voice. I didn't think it possible for someone to be more arrogant than Grenville but low and behold...

"Daphne wants exactly what she can't have, which is us. She'll do or say anything to get her claws in because she's a jealous little cunt." Okay... what am I hearing? A thousand new questions pop into my head.

"What are you blabbering about now?" I try to act like I haven't been hanging on his every word, echoing the non chalonce I see Grenville do so well.

"Long story short- I fucked Daphne. I fucked her so well that it drove her insane, so insane that she stalked me for years. It was a whole thing, but I can't say I blame her. I am irresistible, wouldn't you say?" His eyes flash to mine in the mirror and I give him the middle finger back.

"They say Dreams are wishes your heart makes, let's just say Daphne wants me dead for dumping her and Benji dead for, well just being a prick, I guess? Why does she hate you again? Don't tell me you fucked her too?" I smirk at his nickname for Grenville.

"She hates me because I told her I would murder her and her entire family without blinking if she kept pursuing you," he says with a sigh. *What the fuck is this family?*

"Can we stop for food, I'm hungry," I say, changing the subject. If I pry anymore it'll make me look like I'm pumping them for information. Then again, who knows if they're telling me the truth? Isn't this one big messy web of lies at this point? I'll stash the information away anyway, I know I'll be heading straight for the library once we're back. I'll make it my life's mission if I have to find out exactly what this family's secrets are.

THE HOUSE OF GRENVILLE

WHEN WE ARRIVE BACK at the university, they both offer to escort me back to my room but I refuse, dying to get stuck in my own research and already knowing the girls will be waiting to integrate me as soon as I walk through the door and I haven't thought of how to hide the horrors I'd witnessed yet.

"The walk will do me good, but thanks. I'll see you around, Zach." I give him a tight lipped smile and turn away dragging my suitcase

"What, no thank you for defending your honour? You wound me Louisa!"

I smirk at his sarcasm before turning back and saying,

"My apologies, thank you for giving my nightmares enough fuel to terrify me for a lifetime." I head inside, not bidding goodbye to Grenville, determination fueling my every step towards the emerald wing.

I pass the eerie portraits whose eyes seem to follow my every step in their golden gilded frames. Once I close the door to my room, I listen closely for the sound of the girls. I hear nothing, pure silence. *Bliss*. I put the suitcase on my bed and throw the window open, basking myself in the nippy November breeze.

It will be christmas soon and I can't wait to see the grounds blanketed in soft white snow. I take a deep breath, filling my lungs with fresh air. It's only then that I let my walls down as I start to compartmentalise everything I had witnessed. Once the tears start, I can't stop them and I let myself sink into the armchair where he had once sat and curl myself up into a ball. I've swapped one devil for another, this one with more power than I could possibly imagine. *"They say that dreams are a wish that your heart makes"* Why had I dreamt of him? Was I that sexually frustrated? I barely know him and yet my subconscious seems to be drawn to him like a dog in heat, it didn't seem to give a fuck that he murdered someone right in front of me. I didn't feel afraid when I saw them again in the hotel room, despite knowing that what they did was wrong.

I dry my eyes, my mind made up as I make my way over to the bathroom to freshen myself up. I have to think of a way out of this deal, to put as much distance between myself and them as I possibly can. Dad will just have to wait where he is for now.

Once I've scrubbed myself clean and thrown on a pair of leggings and a knitted oversized jumper, I grab my backpack and make a beeline for the Library.

What I need is blackmail. I need to discover a secret big enough that if I threaten him with it, he'll end the deal with no questions asked.

Chapter 24:

I've spent a total of 3 weeks trying to gain access to the Grenville family history, with absolutely no success. I've guessed that he'd be a step or two ahead of me, but to close the section entirely and to have it patrolled? Either he's paranoid or my hunch was right, there must be something damning hidden in those archives.

After week two, instead of simply trying to walk in, I make myself at home at one of the desks near it to watch and see if the guard takes any breaks. To my disappointment, he takes none. No matter how long I stay there, he never leaves his post. On the plus side, this also gives me nothing else to do in there but study.

I am way ahead of where I should be thanks to my ability to retain information quickly, which has me bouncing down to the lecture hall to hand the politics professor my essay. But when I walk in, my stomach drops as I look at the familiar face standing in his place. Zach Grenville.

He's dressed to the nines and flirting with some blonde bimbo that I recognise as the girl from Oxford that Bella and Cora had seen off at the rugby game. Why the fuck are they both here?

"What are you doing here?" I ask and they both turn to me.

Zach's expression is cold, like I've never met him before, like I didn't see him murder someone for insulting me.

"Ah yes, my brother's girlfriend. I wondered if I'd get you in my class. I'm told you're extraordinarily intelligent, despite your background. Do you have your essay for me to look at?"

I'm dumbfounded, why is he acting like this? I hand him my essay and try to remain professional despite my nervous system telling me to punch his smug face.

"Thank you, lectures aren't happening today so you can see yourself out."

He doesn't take his eyes off Grenville's ex and my blood boils even more. How dare he dismiss me like this, for her too nonetheless. Wait, *why do I care?* I've known the bloke for all of about 5 minutes. Fine, if that's how he wants to play it, I'll pretend he doesn't exist right back.

I turn on my heels and leave them to their pretty whispers and smiles. Once the door closes behind me, I stand in the empty corridor for a moment, wondering why nobody else came to the lecture. I hadn't received an email or anything, I wonder if anyone else did. Zach probably didn't send it to me on purpose. I start texting the group chat to see if the girls know why that bimbo has been transferred here, my feet moving towards the library before I know what I was doing. I guess that's where I'm going, to stare at the Grenville section for four fucking hours.

When I get to the library, I dump my stuff on the table I've come to call mine, then go through my normal routine of getting myself set up with my work. I lay out my two notebooks, one for thoughts, one for facts and I space them on either side of me. Then I lay out my highlighters in the form of a perfectly pastel rainbow. Some may say this is sad, but I call it a happy workspace. Setting my laptop down in between the notebooks, I open it up and finally glance up to see the security guard's chair empty. *What are the chances?* My heart leaps and I get up slowly from the table.

My footsteps are lighter than a feather but my breathing sounds like a rabid animal. I focus on it as I edge forward towards the place that hopefully holds all of the answers. I pop my head around and down the aisle to confirm it's empty. I don't know how long I have so I step over the chain without hesitation and start to scour the titles of the books.

My mind laps up the titles, processing the dates, reeling at what I might find here.

How far back could these secrets be? I remember his dad saying something about "this is the price of being a Grenville," but I'm certain that was to do with the marriage he was so opposed to. Deciding that I probably have about two more minutes at the most, I grab the oldest and newest book I can see. Now I know the time the guard is away, I can always come back. *Will he notice two books missing? Shit, probably. I mean he has nothing better to do than stare at them all day.* Climbing back over the chain, I tiptoe to my seat, shoving the heavy books in my bag. I quickly walk down the aisles looking for books similar in length and colour. I grab a thick old looking brown book which is about the Cold War and an even older one about Henry the eighth's secret love child. Hurrying back to the forbidden aisle, relieved to see the guard still gone, I place the decoy books in the gaps on the shelves and step back and admire my handy work. I'll have to stay up all night to get them back in time tomorrow but that's not an issue.

I smugly walk back to my desk and sit down, looking around to make sure I'm the only person in this section. Pulling up a webpage with some bullshit about "Power vs Corruption," I try my hardest to study it like my life depends on it. I am usually here for 3-4 hours, it has become my new routine and the woman at the front desk might notice if I left now.

I stare at the screen, willing to put Grenville and the books to the back of my mind until later, but the curiosity is burning me from the inside out. I start making notes on the topic anyway, "Power VS Corruption by Louisa Garrick," but my hand stills as I hear footsteps approaching. I turn around expecting to see the security guard but nobody is there. I definitely heard someone. I furrow my brows and say a stupid, "Hello?" which comes out pathetically faint.

I turn back to the laptop, trying to concentrate, but a prickling on the back of my neck makes me grow uneasy. I glance over my shoulder again and see nothing. I stand up and start gathering my stuff into a neat pile when a familiar voice makes me jump out of my skin, "Going somewhere, Garrick?" he asks. I jolt forward from the shock, my legs knocking against the table.

"Jesus Christ, Grenville. What's wrong with you?" I say, putting a hand over my heart as if that will still it. I survey his all black suit and freshly cut hair, he looks like he did the first day here.

"The librarian tells me you're here every day for hours, I want to know why." His tone is sharp and his eyes are like steel, and from that alone I know that my hunch is right. Something is buried here, something he doesn't want me to know.

"It's quiet here, away from the other students and it lets me focus better." I swallow and I know it's given away my lie by how his eyes dart down to my throat and watch it bob.

"More lies," he hisses.

"Now tell me why you're here next to the section of my family's history."

He closes the space between us within a few strides, his silver eyes staring into mine searching for the truth. I know if I tell a lie he'll have my head for it, I don't know how but he always seems to know when I'm lying.

"I... wanted to see you again," I splutter, looking down at my feet.

"I thought you might come back here one day and I was hoping if I studied here I'd bump into you."

My cheeks heat and I chew my lip. It is the truth, partially anyway. I haven't seen him since leaving him outside of the university the day we got back. He's been in no lectures, I've not seen him at any dinners; that love sick teenager inside of me still holds onto the fact that perhaps one day he'll care for me.

He grabs my chin roughly and lifts my head up to meet his eyes. His expression is softer, now that I've betrayed my biggest vulnerability- he now knows that I care.

"You know what this is, it can never be anything more. No matter how much you, or I want it to be."

My brows furrow, what did he just say?

"What is it about you that gets under my skin so much? No matter how hard I try to keep you at a distance, I can't seem to stay away from you."

My heart explodes, filling me with something warm and comforting, something I haven't felt in a very long time.

"Then don't." I say, taking a bold step towards him and placing a hand on his chest.

"Why can't we just be two people, who aren't in different social standings. Why can it not be that simple? I'm not asking for a marriage. I'm not asking for money. I just want you." He smiles as his hand threads through my hair.

"Because that is the curse of it, don't you see? I can never give you what you want. With me things will never be simple."

I stare into the tormented eyes of Benjamin Grenville, and I wonder what it would be like; to be with him fully, to give him control of everything and let myself fall into his world of silk and silver.

"You're afraid," I say matter-of-factly, "you're afraid of what will happen if you blur those lines between us." I watch as the softness in his face disappears, replaced by the sneering marble exterior that haunts the halls of this place.

"You coward," I spit at him and try to back away but his grip on my hair tightens and he pulls my face towards his. I gasp at the force of it, at the sudden closeness of his breath.

"The only thing I'm afraid of is losing you," he snarls.

"Then prove it," I say, my lips grazing his. His eyes flicker to my lips and I watch them darken.

"You are an infuriating woman," he whispers and then his lips are on mine, hot and brutal as his tongue slips into my mouth.

My hands wrap themselves around the back of his head as I kiss him back, matching his tongue stroke for stroke. There is nothing soft and sensual about this, this is brutal and unyielding. A claiming.

There's no going back now. His lips leave mine bruised and swollen as he starts making his way down my neck. His hands release my head and travel down my body to my waist, leaving a scorching trail of heat in its wake. He takes off my knitted jumper, revealing my emerald green lacy bra before he pushes me backwards until my thighs hit the desk. The next thing I know I'm being hauled on top of it.

My perfectly arranged stationary scatters as I wrap my legs around his waist locking him in place as I kiss him hungrily, the taste of him intoxicating- laced with a sweet poison I'd happily die from. I feel how hard he is as he presses up against me, and I can't get enough. I love that I get this reaction from him. I need more and I need it now. The months of hatred, of frustration and secrets have built up inside of me so much that it feels like I'm about to explode.

He explores every inch of my torso as he unclips my bra with expertise, and rips it away. I gasp for air as he engulfs my breast into his mouth, biting and licking, the pain and pleasure building a euphoric feeling in my stomach.

He wraps his hand around my throat and pushes me down hard onto the desk, as he pulls down my leggings and sends them to the floor. The cold bites at my heavy breasts and I watch his eyes devour me,

"Perfection," he says as he releases my neck and I realise I'd been holding my breath.

His finger hooks onto my knickers and he slides them down, leaving me painfully exposed in front of him. His eyes travel further down and I blush from his gaze, knowing he can see just what he does to me, how much hold he has on me. He undoes his jeans and sets himself free and I marvel at the sheer size of him. He looks into my eyes as if asking for my permission and I manage a nod.

His fingers slide down me and my back arches off the desk with the touch.

"Dripping for me Garrick?" he questions in that delicious way he does.

I moan as his thumb pushes down on my clit and he pushes two fingers inside of me, pumping in and out painfully slow. I grind on his hand as he circles me hard with his thumb.

"Eyes on me," he says and I do as I'm told, I stare into those painfully beautiful eyes of his.

I moan and gasp as my pleasure edges forward, driving me to the brink of insanity, no longer caring who or what I am, or that I'm giving myself to my tormentor.

His fingers still and he pulls them out of me, I let out a whimper as he brings them to his mouth and licks them clean. Then, without warning, he plunges into me in one very hard and brutal thrust causing me to almost buck off the desk from the force of it, my shocked gasp dangling in the air of the silent library.

I moan loudly as he slides in and out slowly, waiting for me to adjust to him, his eyes never leaving mine. His hands grip my thighs tightly as his thrusts become faster and harder. I arch my back and angle my hips in response, pulling him closer with my legs, holding onto him tightly with every fibre of my being.

He hits that sweet spot with every thrust and after a few moments I'm already seeing stars, my moans loud and breathy as I watch him fuck me into oblivion. I clench around him and his moan is a sound that I will do anything to hear again. My world explodes and the relief is overwhelming, he fucks me harder and my leg begin to shake. Bracing a hand on the desk, he spills himself inside of me, collapsing on top of me drenched in sweat.

We lie there for a moment, our breaths ragged and the only sound echoing through the vast room. I run my hands through his hair which he seems to like judging by the small shiver his body makes and I know then that I am his in every way.

Our bubble is soon burst by an old croaky voice that I recognise as the lady from the front desk.

"Mr. Grenville, I'm sorry to disturb you but your father is waiting for you."

But the horror isn't over yet.

"At last we meet, Miss Garrick. I've heard so much about you."

Chapter 25:

There's embarrassment and then there's this. I cover my face as Grenville slides out of me, but doesn't get off. He shields me from view.

"Always were an exceptional cock block, father. I'll be with you momentarily."

I pull my hands away and see him smirking down at me, I don't dare sit up and look around his body. If I can help it, I'll be dressed and out of here as quickly as I can. Once the sound of footsteps teeters away, I let out a groan and grimace. Then he does something that surprises me, he smiles broadly and laughs. I watch as the joy takes over his face, it makes him more beautiful than I've ever seen him. I smile back at him and laugh too, realising this is the first time I've heard it.

His eyes sparkle, as he gazes down at me. "Truly beautiful," he says as he tucks a strand of my hair behind my ear, a gentle movement so foreign to me. "Under any other circumstance I'd escort you back to your room, but I do have a meeting here," he says as he kisses my lips lazily, igniting a thirst for him all over again.

"A perfect gentleman," I hum, before pushing him off and scanning the floor for my clothes. I hop down and throw them back on hastily.

"Those are some big books you've got there, Garrick."

My blood runs cold when I remember exactly what I'd been doing here before he arrived. I pull my jumper down and turn back to do the bag up before he can see what's inside.

"We're still keeping secrets, I see," he says with a huff.

I swing the bag over my shoulder and walk towards him,

"I'll keep mine until you can part with yours." The tantalising promise hangs between us like a dangling carrot on a stick, another line we might cross. But not today.

"I hope your meeting goes well, I'll see you around," I say awkwardly, not quite knowing where we stand with each other.

He gives me a tight smile and smooths his hair back and I turn from him, eager to head back to my room and begin unravelling the mystery surrounding this man.

MY STOMACH GROWLS AS I shut the door and I realise I haven't eaten since breakfast that day. After dumping my heavy backpack in my room, I head back into the kitchen to rifle through the fridge. My mouth waters as my eyes land on a plate of perfectly prepared sushi, which means that Bella wouldn't be far behind.

I pull it out and begin unwrapping it, placing it delicately on a grazing platter, something I'd learned to do in my lessons- how to be the perfect hostess. It started with food, nobody was to know you didn't prepare it- so there was an art into making it look home made by where you place it. It also had to be delightfully instagrammable, so that your guests would create a buzz around being one of your VIP's.

Once I'm satisfied with the placement of everything, I grab the tiny bowls and decant various sauces into each of them. I finish off the table with a vase full of chopsticks and light a few candles. I admire my work, it seemed so silly at the start of all this- learning such trivial things. But as I look at the tiny details on the napkins, I think about how much time and effort I put into it. How much love has gone into it.

I pull out my phone and snap a picture, sending it into the group chat and ordering them to bring champagne with them for lunch. I'm greeted instantly with various approving emojis and I smile as I head back into the bedroom, deciding I'd allow myself a peak of his history.

Pulling out the oldest book dated 1612, I open it up to the first page:

"*In Grenville Genus*" the title reads, great- Latin. The illustration below it is faded and worn. I run my finger down the vines that have wrapped themselves around the familiar coat of arms. The crow stares back at me with its beady eye, as if it knows someone like me shouldn't have access to this. "*Potestas Aeterna.*"

"Eternal power," I say out loud. I flip it over to the next page to find it all written in latin. I impatiently pull my phone back out of my pocket and take a photo of the page, uploading it to an AI translation site. The joys of modern technology.

It takes a while to load, but when it does, I inhale the information greedily:

"*An account written by Sir Frederick Bennetine the king's scribe. 1611 May.*

A family not born of wealth and power, have situated themselves at the right hand of our great king James I. They tell stories of Christ's forbidden chalice, and grab at lands freely given by favour of the king. His majesty, the Uniter of Scotland and England, born of both blood, is eager to begin his search and continues to ransack the royal treasury in his desperation.

His ill health is still secret, a war will come if it is revealed. The throne is still delicate from the cousins bloodshed, I hope one day for simpler and safer times out of the Grenville brothers hands."

"Lou? Are you in there?"

The sound of Cora's voice startles me and I close the book hastily.

"Yes, I'll be out in a moment." I shove the book back into my backpack and slide it under my bed, cursing my friends for interrupting.

The information is here, I know it is. I can only hope that the evening will fly by and I can dive back into it as soon as humanly possible.

Chapter 26:

I'm greeted by the girls' big grins as they flock to the spread of food I've laid out. Bella, of course, is pouring champagne but she stops and narrows her eyes at me as I approach.

"What?" I ask her, shifting nervously under her assessment. Then her eyes widen,

"You had sex, didn't you?" she says accusingly.

My stomach drops, I'd been so wrapped up in the book that it seemed like a lifetime ago, not just an hour, that Grenville ploughed into me on top of a desk. I struggle to find my voice as I scramble through my brain to find some sort of excuse.

"I... did not have sex," I say, but I already know my blush has given me away as they exchange a glance between one another.

"Bella is never wrong! Who did you shag? Grenville's going to be livid when he finds out!" Cora exclaims.

Why would she not think it was Grenville I had sex with?

I yank the glass out of Bella's hand and take a seat opposite them, sighing as I do.

"I... yes, I had sex."

They squeal and I wonder how much of the truth I should tell them. I have so many secrets from them now- I still need to tell them about the Daphne comments from Zach. I can give them this, right?

"Tell us everything!" Bella's eyes gleam as she grabs some chopsticks and starts tucking in like she's watching Saturday night TV.

"I had sex with Grenville."

Their mouths drop.

"In the library."

They continue to stare.

"And his dad interrupted."

Bella chokes on the sushi. I leave it there and watch while Cora pats her vigorously on the back. I say nothing else and let them process the information. I can't help but giggle at their cartoon-like faces.

"How the fuck did that happen?" Bella asks, clutching her chest and gasping for breath.

"I was... in the library looking for a book. I found the book and then Grenville showed up and then... he fucked me on the desk." I chew my bottom lip, awaiting the responses.

Cora screams at the top of her lungs. "Daphne is going to be fucking estatic, this could all be over for you soon, Lou. You've got your hooks in him now- time to sink that miserable ship." I look down at my plate, guilt suffocating me.

"There's something else you need to know, something I need your help with." They frown at my response.

"There's something you need to know about Professor Daphne and I need you to help me find out if it's true or not," I say looking between them, they nod at the same time, intrigue lacing their faces.

I launch into a retelling of what Zach had told me, skipping over the murder details. I watch the wheels turn in their heads and I know that they know something.

"There was talk about how she got the job here, there's no denying she's bloody brilliant but teaching always seemed beneath her. She could walk into a high paying job, no issues with her qualifications and connections, but she chose here instead. The ball tomorrow has some guests from outside the university coming, perhaps Bella and I could do some digging." Bella nods in agreement. "It would explain why she wants to break the political system, especially if his brother is involved somewhere in there." I nod.

"Those were my thoughts too, use me to get to Grenville and destroy the very thing that gives him power and would affect his entire family."

I know I've hit the nail on the head but I need proof if I'm going to get out of this. Daphne doesn't strike me as the type of person who will leave quietly, the exposure would have to be breathtaking.

"What are you wearing tomorrow?" Bella asks, pulling me from the thousands of conspiracies floating in my head.

"I haven't given it much thought if I'm honest," I say dreamily.

"I'm sure Grenville will send you something expensive." She cocks her eyebrow as she takes a swig of her drink.

Right on cue my phone dings from my pocket and I pull it out to see a text from Grenville;

"Do you have a date for tomorrow?"

I smile and respond,

"I have nothing to wear."

Less than 30 seconds later he replies with,

"Nothing is fine with me."

I blush and put my phone away. Cora is wiggling her eyebrows at me and Bella is smirking.

"Let's take the day off tomorrow, I'll have my designer flown in from New York with some options."

I sigh and run my hands through my hair, wondering how my life has become so utterly complicated.

Chapter 27:

I say goodnight to the girls after hours of giggling and comparing dick sizes, a little bit of normality I didn't know I needed has refreshed me for the task ahead. I take a shower, feeling a little sad that I no longer smell like Grenville's skin and settle into bed. I'd made the decision earlier not to read anymore of the book, that my focus is now to be on shady Professor Daphne and exposing her. Even after today's library antics, I still don't know where I stand with him. But I'd definitely fuck it up by betraying his trust and finding out all of his buried family secrets.

I should do what any sane person would do and take the books back down and pray they haven't been missed. As I toss and turn in the bedsheets, the temptation of knowing him better is all too much. So, against my better judgement, I grab the book from under my bed and start to translate the pages again. To my dismay, none of these entries have dates.

"His majesty is driven mad by the promise of the Grenville brothers. A cure for the illness he is succumbing to, he dreams of ruling our great empire for eternity.

The longer Bartholomew stands at his side, the further his poison spreads. The rabid one, one born not of our country whose blood is filth, takes the queen to bed most nights, keeping her occupied away from the king's madness so that Bartholomew might earn more titles and power. The gunpowder plot runs deep in his brain, the paranoid fool. He says his dreams are something a demon gives him, the devil taunts him with it. Silver eyes watch my step and ink, they know I'm close to the truth."

I frown slightly, why would they want this man's diary entries as a testament to their family legacy? "The one born not of this country," I echo the words. What does that mean? Well, I know what it means, but why does this author have to be so cryptic about it?

I skip a few entries further into the book, how did they gain entry to the king's court in the first place? What is it that the Grenville brothers have on all of these wealthy men to keep them in line? More importantly, why is Daphne so interested...

"The winter solstice brings no joy, the parliament that was declared, I demolished after 18 days. I could not allow the silver ones in, to give them total power. I had to do it, he will have my head.

They leave tomorrow for the expedition, it is of utmost secrecy the king only trusts them now. He is too sick to leave, the silver ones are taking a legion of guards to my disappointment."

The silver ones? The eyes. I turn the page only to be met by an all too familiar face. It can't be... I rub my eyes as I stare down at the drawing. It looks just like Grenville, well if he had long hair. The words "Bartholomew Grenville, The Silver One" etched with hatred next to it alongside drops of dried blood. Creepy. *The Apple really didn't fall far from the tree*, I think as I turn the next page and translate the next entry.

"They returned victorious, but empty handed for the king. They claim the chalice could not be moved, the liquid inside that held Christ's blood could not be poured. Some sorcery surrounded it. I warned the king that the devil was at play, not any man could conquer death; it is not God's will to grant it. Anointed by God and in God he must see, must turn to him to see The Silver Ones lies.

They claim they now hold the power of the chalice and will share that power with the king provided the king bends the knee to them. He did so, in front of all nobles, the King declared The Silver Ones as gods, men put on earth to show the true power of Christ and that he would be his servant."

I snort at the passage, this king was clearly mad enough to believe them. So that's how they gained power, they tricked a king into thinking eternal life was palpable. But why would anyone think that now? We have all that technology could offer, his own dad is dying of cancer for fuck sake. Surely if he had the gift of eternal life he'd share it with future generations? I flick to the very last page and translate it on my phone again.

"1649

Charles is dead, they did it. The Silver Ones, the young that stay young. I found them in his chambers, I know it was them. A brutal and bloody murder. I caught one, the one with dark hair and dark skin. I threw him into the dungeons of the tower to watch him rot. The other one fled, but he will be back. I will continue my father's work and keep my promise to destroy the Grenvilles."

"The young that stay young," I say out loud as my brain tries to compartmentalise it all. It's not possible. It defies the laws of nature- of everything we know. My mind reels as the pieces of the puzzle start to fit together, could it be possible that these two brothers are the same brothers from this book?

I fly off the bed and grab a notebook and pen, frantically writing down everything I know, piecing together what I can. I need more information. These are the words of a rambling man with a grudge, how can I take them as the truth? Imagine how insane I'd sound if I approached anyone with this?

I'm hit with an idea that stops me dead in my tracks. I grab my dressing gown from the bottom of the bed and run from my room, making my way to the front door, hands shaking as I twist the silver knob. If this is real, this changes the course of everything. No, of course it's not real. How the fuck could it be?!

But I have to know. I have to find out.

Pulling open the door, I walk down the dimly lit hallway and open my phone's torch to light the way. I walk a little further towards the marble statue, ignoring a prickling sensation on the back of my neck. Like I'm being watched.

I stop at the statue and shine the light up to the portrait that sits above it, the similarities hit me all at once as I survey the scene. A man with shoulder length silver hair and silver eyes stands in front of a crowd in a village. I move closer and see his square jaw, sharp and defined, staring back at me. The crowd is enamoured with him, hanging on his every word like he's God incarnate. When I examine the crowd closer, I find him standing away from it, arms folded across his front, one hand resting on a sword. His long dark hair and tanned skin a contrast to the silver eyes gleaming back. Such detail the painter has poured into this.

    I place my shaking hand on the side of the wall, panting breathlessly as the rational part of my brain remains silent, apparently having no clever words for this. I glance down at the corner of the painting, "1701- The Silver Ones, Trafalgar Square, London".

Chapter 28:

My dreams leave me waking in a cold sweat. Dreams of silver eyes and gleaming teeth, the word I don't want to say out loud- dangles on the tip of my tongue. He was there and then he wasn't, chasing me, tormenting me. The truth is so close, but when I try to touch it, it disappears into smoke.

In the morning, I have to drag myself into the kitchen for coffee. I almost entertained the thought of staying in bed all day, pretending I was sick so that I could avoid this ridiculous ball prep that's about to take place. But I know Bella wouldn't have it, she'd drag me from my bed and then tell me off for lying.

I have no choice but to get through today.

I sit in the glam chair, staring into space, not hearing the conversations happening around me. Everything feels muffled, and unimportant. My phone buzzes from my pocket and I pull it out and answer my brother's call, trying my hardest to sound normal.

"What do you want?" I ask bluntly.

"Is it your time of the month already? Can't a big brother just call to see how his little sister is?" He says cheekily.

"No, you're incapable of such a thing. I'm busy so answer the question," I spit back, examining the French manicure the nail technician has just finished doing. Classy, elegant, goes with every outfit...

"I need your boyfriend to ring me back." I roll my eyes.

"What sort of trouble are you in now that only Grenville can help you with? Gambling? Drugs?" I list off, but he cuts me off before I can continue.

"None of your business, but let's just say if he doesn't get back to me soon he's going to lose a very valued customer." I roll my eyes again.

"He gives you a job in finance, a very well paid one, might I add, and you still find a way to go back to..."

All eyes turn to me and I realise I almost outed him in front of the entire makeup and hair team.

"Old habits," I finish.

"I'm not discussing business with you, baby sister, I've got a job to do and I can't do it without the go ahead of your fancy pants boyfriend. So do me a favour, get your lips off his cock and tell him to..."

I gasp and hang up before he can finish that, my face no doubt bright red.

What business was he doing with him? As far as I know he'd given him a job in one of his offices, quite high up too considering the only qualifications he has is a GCSE in P.E. Frankie had left school at 15, claiming he wanted to be a boxer.

I remember how hard he trained in the Birmingham championships, that was where he met Oscar. Frankie had taken him under his wing and introduced his dad to mine and the rest is history. Then the war for the territories began. Frankie was streetwise, but didnt see how quickly Oscar had climbed the ranks from corner boy to distributor until it was far too late.

The secrets surrounding me just keep piling up, I wonder how long it will be until Grenville trusts me with them. How can I be anything to him without the truth? Then again, I probably am nothing to him. We still haven't had *that* conversation.

My phone buzzes again, a text this time from Frankie-

"Get him to call me back!!"

I sigh and pull up Grenville's number. I hesitate for a moment, should I call him or text him? What if he's busy? Would I be disturbing him too much?

Shaking my head, I wave for the stylist to leave me be.

"I have to make a call," I say to the room, not looking up from his name as I seek out the privacy of my bedroom.

What's the worst that can happen? He won't be able to tell something's off with me just from a phone call, I'm sure of it, right? Then again, if he is in fact an immortal being... Nope, absolutely not, I'm not going down that road.

I tell myself I'll only let it ring four times and if he doesn't answer I'll hang up and text him, but he picks up on the second ring.

"What's wrong?" he asks frantically. The tone catches me off guard.

"Um, hey. Frankie's been blowing up my phone. He wants me to tell you to call him back." I bite my lip, waiting for him to call me out, tell me he knows I stole the books.

"Are you there?" I ask after a few too many beats of silence.

"Yes, I'm just contemplating how pissed off you'd be if I dismembered your brother."

He says it so passively, I grab my little pocket notebook that I'd stayed up writing in last night and write "Seems to have no empathy for human life." in my facts section.

"What did you say?"

I freeze. *Shit.* Did I say that out loud?

"I said," I start, thinking of how to cover my arse, "I'd have no problems ending your... human life? If you did that I mean, my brother is very special to me... I'd, um... I'd not forgive you if you did that. I have to go... curl my bags... no, I mean my hair. I'll see you at the ball. Oh, and thank you for the dress. Please just call him back." I hang up quickly and smack my forehead as I sink into the bed. *What the fuck am I doing?*

THE DRESS IS BEAUTIFUL, the base colour black and decorated with silver brocade that stretches up the puffy skirt and around the bodice. He didn't send a shawl though, something that worries me with how cold it's been. I guess we'll be in the ballroom surrounded by people, so I may be warm enough. *Does he feel the cold?* I think as I step into the dress, the stylist pulling it up around me. It fits like a glove and I wonder how he got my measurements so right. I try to be excited, to get into the spirit of things, but the possibility of him being an immortal being weighs heavy on me. Every movement is an effort, like I'm wading through the deepest of sea. Suffocating.

I stashed my notebook and pen inside my bag and have gone over the plan with Bella and Cora. They know who is in Daphne's closest circle. They've both been meticulous with their research, I'll give them that. But my blood has chilled at the sight of the names, the same people from the dinner party will be there. They all have to be in on the secret, and I'd have to use that to my advantage tonight. Tonight there will be answers.

As we walk down the corridors towards the ballroom, I can't help but notice how different the world feels now. I find myself searching the shadows, terrified of there being a pair of silver eyes glaring back at me. The same feeling from the other night follows us, the chill of it like a gentle caress across my bare shoulders. I don't dare turn back, my brain can't handle the reveal of any other mythical creatures right now.

I focus on each step, gripping tightly to the girl's arms. They both have sensed something has been wrong with me all day but I don't dare confide in them. I don't want their perfect view of the world shattered- I also don't want them to think that I should be locked in an Asylum. I've brushed their comments off and placed the blame on Professor Daphne, making out that shady dealings is what has me on edge which isn't exactly far fetched. However at this point, I view her situation as more of an inconvenience than anything.

I know Cora buys it by the way she nods, but Bella seems to have a sixth sense that is second to none when it comes to this kind of thing. I haven't missed how her eyes narrow at me when she thinks I'm not looking. I wonder if she finds me as infuriating as I find Grenville.

My breath hitches as we enter the Ballroom, it's been completely transformed into a winter wonderland. Fake snow falls from the ceiling in a gentle flurry. The bare trees give the place a woodland feel, decorated with delicate icicles and tiny fairy lights. Then my eyes fall on the centrepiece of the room and I damn near faint. A giant Ice sculpture stands in the middle of the room on a platform, with the unmistakable features of a very old drawing that had haunted my dreams. The original Grenville, or the one in the same?

"I need a drink," I yell over the orchestra, my accent peeping through.

"Agreed," Cora yells back and, as if by magic, a waiter appears holding a tray of champagne.

"Thank you," I say as I take a flute, noticing his woodland fox mask.

I scan the crowd, most of the people here are in some type of animal mask. I look at the girls to see if we're the only ones that didn't get the memo.

"Why aren't we in masks?" I ask them.

"Masks are tacky, I was having nothing ruin this outfit." Bella flips her razor straight, rapunzel length hair behind her back and I snort a little. Typical Bella, her dress is unbelievable though. She'd chosen an emerald green figure-hugging sequin gown, a corset style top baring her shoulders and complimenting her beautiful tanned skin so well. But the bottom? She did have to walk like a penguin due to it being so tight but it was worth it.

"You know, Lou, if you want an arse like mine I can give you my plastic surgeon's number." She winks at me playfully and I giggle.

"Ready to divide and conquer?" Cora asks as she fiddles with the pewter blue shawl wrapped around her arms.

"Perhaps soon we could attend one of these things and actually have fun together?" I say as I try to ignore the butterflies dancing in my stomach. Once I crack Daphne, the rest will follow, I'm sure of it. Perhaps then I will be able to confide in my friends, maybe I won't seem so fucking crazy if they figure it out themselves too. Maybe I am just crazy, maybe the trauma of having a family like mine has finally loosened that screw.

I watch the two beautiful women disperse, quiet determination lacing their steps as they approach the different groups congregated around the room. I catch the eyes of the Viscount's wife, standing alone next to the sculpture, she curtseys and dips her head. Maybe now is the time to put Daphne's manipulation skills to the test, perhaps she won't need much of a push if she's still grieving for her husband. Could she be a weak link?

"Viscountess, it's wonderful to see you again. I'm sorry we didn't get a chance to speak at the dinner a few weeks ago." Her left eye twitches at the memory. Perfect.

"My apologies, Miss Garrick. I meant no offence, I'm always very busy at these events," she says, plastering a sweet smile across her face and I feel my patience wearing thin already.

"I was deeply saddened to hear of your husband's recent passing. How are you coping?" I ask, feigning concern.

"Diana, come and meet the new Jockey, we all know you can't resist a flutter on the horses." The voice startles me and the blood drains from my face as I turn and see the Viscount Turnbole in perfectly good health calling his wife from across the room. What the fuck?

"As you can see, Miss Garrick, I don't know what you're talking about."

The grin she shows me is nothing less than evil before she leaves me standing alone. I wrap my arm around my stomach, as if it would help to keep my food down. I make quick strides towards the open french doors that lead out to the veranda.

What the fuck is going on? He's alive? Who else in this fucking room knows about this? What are these people?

The fresh air makes my head spin and I brace myself against the balcony, looking out onto the perfectly trimmed hedges of the maze in the distance. If the Viscount is alive and well then he must be like the Grenville brothers, an immortal being. How could he be? How could any of this be true?

I scramble at the bits and pieces of information I've gathered, trying to fit it all together. Benjamin Grenville is the master puppeteer, the power these fuckers have in the political system are all inherited. Or are they the same, just like him? But if they hold the same immortality power then why are they so afraid of the Grenvilles? What do they have to lose if they can't die either? By their reactions at the dinner, they must all know and be a part of it. Nobody batted an eyelid at the sudden violence because they understood that he'd come back.

Then it clicks. That's what Daphne wants. To be like them, to repeat history over and over, staying in power like the rest of them. I whirl back and look into the ballroom, my eyes widening in horror, it's as if a veil has been lifted. I watch the Grotesque old faces with decaying skin and sallow eyes, laugh and sneer and clink their champagne glasses together. I commit every face to memory. This is unnatural.

"Well aren't you a smart little thing?" A leering voice calls from beside me, my bones chilling at the sound of it.

I clench my hands and turn to face Zach Grenville, dressed so finely that the devil himself would feel inadequate next to him. Why isn't he like the others? His face is the same. There's nothing different about him.

He's leaning a few feet away, staring up to the sky, the full moon casting him in a pearlescent light, so beautiful. How long has he been here? His smirk is devastating.

"I could smell your fear as soon as I got here."

My eyebrows knit together in confusion, his lips didn't move. He saunters closer to me, closing the distance between us and surrounds my senses with his scent. My body screams at me to run, but I'm frozen, basking in the scent of him. He smells like a cold winter's night, like a snow kissed wind dancing between pine trees. Deadly yet comforting.

My head tilts to the side as I fully take him in, like it's the very first time I've seen him. Wait, *his lips didn't move.*

"Your inner monologue is delicious by the way, Benji said you were strong willed but not enough to keep me out." He taps the side of his head as his voice bounces around my brain and the world around me grows dark.

I gasp and open my eyes. All around me is darkness, the kind that has no beginning or end. This darkness is everything and yet nothing. *Am I dead?*

I grab my arm and pinch myself, hard. But don't feel it. I bring my hand up in front of me to test how dark it is, but I can't even see the outline of it. I brace myself before I slap myself hard across the face, but yet again, I don't feel it. *I am most definitely dead.*

"I could search every memory in here you know, that's how powerful I am. Yet, when you look at me, you're not afraid. Which I find curious." Zach says and I spin around towards the sound of the voice but see nothing. I'm met with darkness once again.

"GET OUT OF MY HEAD!" My scream echoes and I fall to my knees as the piercing sound cuts through me like a knife. I feel the hard stone collide with my bones but there's no pain. His laughter swirls around me and I dig my nails into the ground, willing myself to bleed, to feel anything. I can't be in my own head with him, I can't. He'll know. He'll find out what I did.

"Now that is intriguing, what exactly is it you don't want me to find out? I doubt anything would surprise me at this point, I am over 400 years old."

His breath dances across the side of my face and I scream again,

"GET OUT, GET OUT, GET OUT.!"

Then it's like I'm swimming, being dragged up by something through deep murky water. I kick my feet as a tiny slither of light comes into view. I will myself to be faster. Stronger. I need to reach it. I can't breathe. I can't think.

I take a big deep breath as I open my eyes, searching frantically at my surroundings. I'm in his arms. He has me wrapped up tight, shielding me from the cold with his body heat. I let out a small sob, grabbing the side of his face with my hands. Feeling the smoothness beneath my fingers. His eyes close at my touch,

"Please, tell me I'm wrong. Lock me up and tell me I'm insane." My voice cracks as I search his face. He opens his eyes again, they swirl as he clutches me tighter and his brows furrow.

"I'm sorry," he says as tears fall from his eyes.

I clutch at his face digging my nails into his skin. I do it until I draw blood, but he doesn't flinch. I peel away my hands and watch in disbelief as the tiny cuts knit back together just as a single drop of blood escapes from the fresh wound, the only trace that I had hurt him at all.

"Stay away from me!" I shout as I retreat from him, hurt flashes in his eyes as I scramble backwards.

"Don't do this," he says, getting to his feet.

"Louisa, I can explain everything but you can't do this here. Please let me explain."

I flinch at the sound of my name, the first time he's called me it. My heart sinks when I know it will be the last.

"Why not here?" I say as I get to my feet. "Everyone here knows, don't they?" I say accusingly, but he says nothing.

"Do my friends know?" I run my hands through my hair as the questions spill out. "Who else is like you?".

"I can explain, please come with me..." He reaches out his hand and I back away again.

"Don't touch me," I snarl. "You lied, lied about everything."

His gaze hardens and I feel a trickle of fear travel down my spine, before I know what I'm doing, I'm running. Down from the veranda, sprinting past the rose bushes that are flourishing for the last time. I kick my shoes off and hike up my skirts, cringing at the gravel thrashing at my skin. I don't care that I'm panting like a dog, I keep going. I'm at the maze entrance in a second, throwing myself into it and hurling myself around corner after corner, the branches scratching at my bare arms. When I can't stand the stinging in my lungs any more I stop, my legs buckling beneath me as I drop once more to the ground and sob. I clutch at the diamonds clasped around my neck and rip them off in frustration, throwing them as far as I can.

How can any of this be real? How could I have been so foolish? How could I have given myself to a man full of secrets. Secrets so deadly that it would crumble society as we know it if the masses found out. I put my hand in front of my mouth, muffling the sobs escaping me.

I could run, but he knows where my family are. He set them up for life, why? Why would he do that? Why would he do any of it? I hear voices approaching and I spring to my feet, walking quietly to hide behind a hedge. Just as I'm concealed, the voices grow louder, but it's not the ones I was suspecting.

"I'm glad you came to me with this, Cora, you can always trust me with your concerns," Professor Daphne says as she comes into view. *What the fuck?*

I stop breathing for a second as I watch her and Cora come to a stop a little way away from where I'm hidden.

"Can I trust you? Really?"

I raise my eyebrows at her tone, *is she calling her out?*

"I don't believe a word that comes out of your mouth. You blackmailed Bella and me into helping you with Louisa and I want to know why. She's a deer in the headlights, she wasn't cut out for this. Maybe that's why you chose her, you thought she would be easy to control. You knew that Benjamin wouldn't have looked at her twice unless you made her a person of interest. You couldn't give a shit if Louisa gets hurt in the process of your revenge tactics.." Cora steps closer to her and bares her teeth.

"My father will be very interested to know where his very large donation to the school has gone. I could make anything up you know, I could destroy your career in a split second and not even blink."

I gasp a little, shocked at seeing this side of her. Shocked at how far my friend is willing to go to protect me. Cora turns to walk off but Daphne grabs the back of her hair and slams her face down to the floor. I watch in horror as her hands wrap themselves around Cora's throat, cutting off her air supply. "You stupid girl. You haven't been paying attention. Wasn't one of my first lessons about not showing your hand too early? The second was to never turn your back on an enemy..." She squeezes harder and I watch Cora's legs thrash as she tries to gain some purchase.

Panic rises up inside me, I don't know if Cora is like him. Will she come back like the Viscount? I glance around me, deciding I have to do something. I look down and see a large jagged rock hidden beneath the hedge next to me, I grab it and run over towards them, praying I reach her in time as I watch her legs start to still.

"You will not get in my way of immortality, Corinthia," Daphne spits, just as I raise the rock high above my head and bring it down with a sickening thud onto Professor Daphne's head.

It's a peculiar thing, to hold someone's life in your hands. The sound of her shattering skull pierces the silent maze.

Cora gasps roughly and stares up at me wide eyed as she clutches my arms.

"Shhh, it's okay," I say to her, smoothing her head the way my mother used to when I had had a nightmare. Her eyes dart to Daphne and I hear a faint shuffling sound. I turn just in time to see her lunge for me, a silver knife in her hand. But I'm too quick. I dodge out of the way and she slices thin air. Cora retreats back with as much strength as she can muster.

Daphne brandishes the knife at me again, her knuckles white from how hard she grips it. I stare at the blood dripping down her face and her eyes turn glassy, I don't have long before she bleeds out. If I want answers, it's now or never.

"Why? Why me? If you lie to me I will make sure that it's the last lie you ever tell."

The threat dangles between us as her eyes dart around, trying to figure out which way she should run. She throws her head back in maniacal laughter,

"You haven't even begun to scratch the surface. You know nothing. You don't know what they're capable of, what I've seen them do. You had one fucking job and you still screwed it up. But what else could I expect from such low born filth? All I asked was that you entrance him. Make him blind so that he wouldn't see that I'm trying to bring them all down. You know what they are, don't you?" She steps towards me with the knife hanging down at her side.

"We could still do it, you know, we could put a stop to it all. All you have to do is find out where they hide it. We could destroy it together." She has a look of insanity about her as she pleads with me. I glance back at Cora, to my relief she looks confused. I don't think she has a clue.

I could agree, turn around, go back inside and hear him out. Continue this ridiculous charade. But I can't. I *care* about him. The relief at my admission washes over me like the gentle caress of a calm sea. I don't want to destroy him. Even if I did, I want it on my terms.

"You fool," she spits at my hesitancy and my mouth curls into a wicked smile I never knew I was capable of as the glint of the silver knife catches my eye.

I'm not the same girl that came here, no, but what I have cannot be taught. It's a gift that's carved from trauma, the fight or flight that you live in when you spend your life looking over your shoulder. I have something she will never have. Birmingham.

I dodge her lazy attempt at stabbing me with ease as my feet fall into the dance my brother had taught me in the boxing ring all those years ago. She stumbles as she misses and I take full advantage by catching her arm and bending it backwards, twisting hard until I hear a crack reverberate from the hedges.

We're so deep in the maze that the moon is our only source of light, Daphne swings the arm holding the knife aimlessly around as if she might catch me by chance. I let her wear herself out before kneeing her in the groin, causing her to buckle and the knife to leave her hand as she holds out her arms to brace for impact. I press my knee hard into the side of her face as she sobs. The sound is intoxicating, a bloodlust my brother says we're cursed with. I'd denied it my entire life, until my 16th birthday when everything had gone horribly wrong.

"Let me go," Daphne snarls, but I just push harder.

I want to make her hurt, want her to feel it. Every ounce of my anger at the world is pouring into her as she thrashes beneath me.

"You tried to kill my friend, then you tried to kill me. Big fucking mistake." I lean in close to her ear and whisper,

"I'm going to make sure you never hurt anyone again."

Her eyes widen with horror as I toy with her. Grabbing the knife she dropped, the coldness of the silver bites at my skin, I clutch the handle tightly. I grab a fistful of that perfect hair and yank her head up roughly to expose her throat.

"Lou!"

A voice that seems far away shouts, but it's quiet compared to the rage in my ears. I slice through Daphne's throat like it's a block of butter and watch the blood spray the white gravel stones. So much blood.

I feel euphoric. That bloodthirsty part of me that I'd buried on my sixteenth birthday feels sated for the first time in a long time. I revel in the feeling, feeling good, so good, just for a moment before my conscience kicks in.

The screaming gradually reaches my ears, starting off like the voice from before, far away. Then it grows louder, the ringing stops and the blade falls from my hand with a deafening clang as my insides turn into a ravenous storm.

It's Cora that's screaming, I'd forgotten she was here. I was too wrapped up in my own sick head. I drop Daphne's body and stumble back but it's not her anymore. The face distorts and changes until I see my own lifeless eyes staring back at me. "Murderer" the body says.

"No, I, I didn't, I couldn't," I stutter at myself as I retreat backwards from the river of blood coming towards me.

"I... I didn't mean to. I didn't mean to." My own scream rolls through the maze, reaching every hidden crevice inside the hedges.

"You... You didn't mean to, Lou, I saw what happened. You had no choice, she was going to kill us." Cora's warm hands grasp the sides of my face and she forces me to look at her and away from the blood. I pant and clutch at her dress with my blood-soaked hands as I wail and scream.

"Get it together, repeat after me. You had no choice. She had you backed against a corner and tried to stab you. You acted in self defence."

Her words feel like poison, seeping through my bloodstream, driving away what little goodness was left in me. I am not good. I've never been good. I let my Dad go to prison for me, promising I'd never do this again. I've broken that promise, broken everything. *Everything good I touch turns to ash.*

A hard slap across my face forces me from my self loathing.

"Louisa, there are people coming. You need to get it together. Let me do the talking, okay? I'll fix this, it's my fault. You were defending me because I didn't know how to defend myself. Let me fix this, please?"

I stare into her round, light blue eyes, how is she so calm and collected? She just watched me murder someone. I hesitate before I glance down at the body again, terrified of it being my own face again, but I only see the woman I had once idolised staring blankly up at the stars. I collapse into Cora, my sobs uncontrollable, my shaking so violent, my teeth chatter. Footsteps sound through the Maze.

"Fetch me Benjamin Grenville, his fiance's been attacked!"

My body goes rigid as her words float through my brain, my eyes widening in horror. "Fiance?" I breathe out, looking at her as I hear a gasp from my left and the footsteps retreat.

"The only way we're going to get out of this is with his help, there's only so far my fathers power reaches," she mutters under her breath quickly.

"What have you done?" I manage to croak out.

"Saved your life, and mine. Now maybe go back to being hysterical, it'll make this easier to believe."

Easier?

"No, I deserve whatever punishment they see fit. Do you have any idea what you've just done?" I search her eyes and it's then that I know for certain that she has no idea about the truth of the Grenville's.

"You just signed my life away."

Chapter 29:

I stand numbly next to Daphne's body. Cora weaves her tale to the police officers, she should be nominated for an oscar for this performance. The police watch me intently as she speaks, their lips drawn into a sympathetic line as they assess me. It's only when she mentions my last name that one of the officer's ears prick up a little, his face turns inquisitive. If I had powers like Zach, I'd be able to delve into his mind to see exactly what story he was piecing together. If by some chance he has heard of me and my family, he knows all about the signature Garrick temper.

We are famous for their "act now, think later" attitude when it comes to violence. I am the first female born into my family in over 100 years, the mothers that married Garrick men passed down stories of a gypsy curse once put on us. It is said that they would bear no daughters, for if they did, that woman would be their undoing. Women are something different, a gift from Mother Nature herself; men are just there to lend a helping hand. A Garrick woman would be a force to be reckoned with.

I stare at him, wondering if he can see what creature lurks beneath my skin. If he knows I am more like my psychotic father than my nurturing mother. Maybe he's a local and has heard of the curse. He looks old enough that he might have known my grandfather.

A warm hand caresses my cheek, dragging my attention away from Cora's animated story, I'm met with shining grey eyes as I turn.

"Fiance is it?" he says in a low voice, his face etched with concern as he tries to smooth the lines creasing in my forehead.

"I'll never marry you," I spit quietly, and he gives me a cocky grin that makes my stomach tighten.

"Looks like you owe me two now, Garrick, so I think you'll do exactly as I tell you from now on."

There it is. My future. A future controlled by an immortal being. A shiver slithers down my spine as his finger runs down my face to my throat. I swallow hard and my breathing picks up beneath his gentle caress.

"You'll be coming back with us tonight, to our manor," he says as his eyes flick down to my lips, just for a split second.

How can this man even be thinking of fucking me at a time like this?! I'm covered in blood and I'm a sweaty, crying mess.

"I'm not going anywhere with you," I whisper growl at him.

His eyes turn cold and hard as they meet mine.

"I own you, Louisa."

My name sounds like a purr on his lips, for a moment I forget who I am and everything I've done. Then his words hit me like a train.

"I will make you a promise then," I say, my voice dripping with danger.

"I will make every single day of your life a miserable one, no matter how long or short that will be. For however long you intend to keep me under your thumb, I will fight you every single day and I will not rest until your life lies in tatters at your feet."

His mouth tilts into a side grin that makes him look like a mirror image of Zach.

"I can drag her for you, brother, if you wish it. You know I don't mind getting my hands dirty."

I whirl around at the sound of his voice, terror rippling through me as I remember the darkness he tormented me in. Would he take me back there just to get my physical body back to their manor? *Shit this is not good.*

"Good, at least you have the decency to look afraid. Now come on, we're done here."

He tilts his head, gesturing for me to follow him but I stay rooted to the spot.

"I haven't given my statement yet." I say defiantly.

"I did it for you, now hurry up." He pops the P as he turns and walks past the police officers in two long strides, not even stopping to thank them. I glance at Cora and give her a small smile which she returns. My heart aches as I wonder if I'll ever see her again. I have no idea what the Grenville brothers have in store for me at their manor, but now I know who they really are and what they're capable of- the possibilities are endless.

I hesitantly follow Zach, hoping I can keep up and not get lost in the maze. Everything from an hour ago feels like it's from a different life, like a foggy memory that just dances beneath the surface of my consciousness. Easy to grab but quick to flit away if I try.

I keep my head down as I pass the policeman that seemed intrigued hearing my name, not daring to look up at him in case he sees the truth written across my face. That I killed her and I liked it. I liked the feeling of her life slipping away beneath my hands. I liked being in control of it all. *A psychologist would have a field day with me.*

Zach stays five paces in front of me, I have to almost jog to keep him in my line of sight as he weaves his way through the maze with ease. He waits for me at the exit and holds out his arm for me to take, just like he did all those weeks ago.

"So now you want to be a gentleman? What happened to giving me the cold shoulder?" I ask him, folding my arms.

"There are cameras everywhere thanks to your rampage, next time you decide to go on a killing spree, be a little more discreet, will you?"

He looks back towards the Grenville building, arm still offered expectantly. There's no sign of that usual playfulness he holds with me.

I sigh and wrap my arm around his as we begin our walk back up the hill towards the University.

"Are you afraid?" he asks, still not looking at me.

"No," I answer, not sure which fucked up situation he's referring to.

"That means you've killed before."

I notice it's a statement, not a question. Well if he can get into my head so easily anyway I may as well be honest.

"Yes," I say curtly.

"You may survive us yet, Louisa." My head snaps up to face him, tears threatening to spill over again.

"I don't deserve to survive. I'm nothing like the two of you." He gives a laugh that doesn't reach his eyes, for a moment he looks practically melancholy.

"You'll soon understand that there is no such thing as good and evil, we are primal creatures at our core. We do what we have to in order to survive. The sooner you accept yourself for who you are, the funner life becomes."

Is he trying to make me feel better? If he is, he's doing a shitty job of it.

"No, what I did was unnecessary. I lost control and I deserve to be locked up and the key thrown away."

"The option is yours. I won't stop you from marching back into that maze and admitting that you killed Daphne. With me, It will always be your choice."

I look up at him again and furrow my brows.

"I've been around long enough to know that you can't control everything, no matter how hard my brother tries. So why should I waste my time trying to stop you?"

I say nothing else as we walk back up to the balcony and into the ballroom. There's no music now, just a lot of chatter that all stops as everyone turns when they see me walk in. Some look at me in disapproval, others with respect as I walk through them on the arm of a loose cannon.

I meet Bella's eyes, she looks horrified as she starts to rush forward to ask me what happened. I shake my head subtly at her, stopping her in her tracks. *I'll explain everything* I think towards her, hoping that I'm conveying it enough non-verbally. Zach leads us out of the ballroom and into the entrance of the University,

"Do I get to change and wash the blood off of me?" I ask.

"No, there's no time," he says simply.

"I need my things, my phone and laptop..." He holds up a hand to stop me.

"It's all in the car, Benji was planning on bringing you home with us for Christmas anyway."

I snort. "Now I don't get to see my family at Christmas?" I shout at him as I fold my arms across my chest.

"Easy killer," he says, holding up his hands like a white flag, his eyes gleaming at me as he smirks.

Then Zach spins on his heels and walks out the front door, leaving me standing there like an idiot. I follow quickly behind him as I hear the chatter in the ballroom grow louder towards me. *Fine, I'll do as you say, but only so I can figure out a way to rip your head from your body.*

"Get in the car, Louisa, there's plenty of time to plot your revenge on us."

His voice in my head startles me, how did he manage to do that? Can he hear all thoughts? Can he hear what I'm saying right now?

"Only when I want to. I'm not a complete arsehole, I don't dive in whenever I feel like it. I respect people's privacy, unlike you."

"What's that supposed to mean?"

"I hear you stole something very valuable from us."

I roll my eyes in response, he can't possibly think that reading a history book is an invasion of privacy?

Getting into the car, I try to keep my mind blank and away from the questions burning on my lips. I want to hear it from *him* first.

Chapter 30:

I don't remember falling asleep in the back of the Rolls Royce, I wake to the feeling of strong muscular arms wrapped around me. I keep my eyes closed and nuzzle into the hard chest next to my head, a wave of calmness seeping through me. Until I notice movement, I'm being moved- carried. I inhale and drown in the unfamiliar scent that reminds me of a sunny winter day. I feel peaceful. There are no worries plaguing me, no family burdens, no Grenville drama and no dreams of blood speckled gowns in the moonlight.

A cold wave of nausea plunges through me as I jerk awake in a panic,

"Easy killer, don't make me fuck around with your mind again."

I open my eyes at the sound of Zach's smooth voice, his face is stern as he carries me through a house I've never seen before.

"Put me down." I say as I beat his chest like a child throwing a tantrum.

"Okay, killer." Then he drops his arms releasing me from the warmth of his embrace and I fall straight on my arse onto the cold marble floor. I squeak on impact and throw him my deadliest look. Zach flicks a spec of invisible dust from his black suit jacket.

"You don't have to be so rough about it," I huff out as I scramble to my feet, the cold marble biting at my bare toes. Then I remember. I remember why I'm here and all that has happened, it comes back faint, in bits and pieces. Running from him and the darkness, the hedges being so tall the moon could barely light my way. The blood that flowed out of Professor Daphne's neck. I clutch at my chest as if that will help slow my heart rate as the memories slam into me.

"Come on, Killer, don't make me drag you by your pretty little feet." I stumble as I retreat from him and my back hits the staircase pillar, I put my hands behind me and clutch at the wood, wishing I could disappear into the grain.

"Stop calling me that," I say between ragged breaths.

He smirks and cocks an eyebrow as he dares a step towards me.

"Fine, find your own way to your room then. I must mention the ghosts though, the place is practically bursting with them." He grins devilishly as he begins to climb the stairs casually. Taking a quick look around, I search for threats lurking in the shadows. The place is dark, lit only by candlelight much like the university. It isn't as big but it follows the same style, gothic with an air of arrogance that fits these two immortal beings. I don't feel like taking my chances on yet another supernatural discovery today, so I hesitantly follow him up the stairs.

My calves ache as I climb the second set, the exhaustion finally setting in from the last 24 hours. Gripping tightly onto the bannister, I silently wish I'd let him carry me. When I reach the top, I find myself in a small area that looks very much like a waiting room, a deep red settee sits comfortably on the back wall flanked by two marble carvings of -thankfully- nobody I recognise. A moody painting of a deserted lake sits above it, to either side there are two very heavy looking doors. Zach is leaning next to the one on the right, judging me vicariously as I take it all in. *At least there's no creepy portraits.*

"His room or mine?" he asks with a wicked grin.

I scoff and walk towards the other door, wanting nothing but space from this arsehole.

"Mine? Perfect!" he says gleefully, stopping me just before I touch the handle. Shooting him a look, I sigh.

"Zach, I'm not in the mood for your games."

"You're no fun, here's me thinking you were just getting interesting."

He's a little too close for comfort as he reaches around me, grazing my waist and unlocking the door, swinging it open on creaky hinges.

"Sweet dreams." He flashes me with a grin and I swallow at the threat, darting into the room and closing the door behind me quickly.

I wait for a moment, gathering myself before I turn around, bracing my hand against the old wood. I hadn't realised that silence could be so suffocating, I wonder if perhaps I've gone deaf. I tap against the wood just to make sure. It's too quiet, I need to occupy my mind before Grenville gets here. Will he sleep in here? Will he tell me everything tonight? Will he tell me at all or am I supposed to keep guessing and researching?

I killed someone.

How am I supposed to rationalise my feelings for him now that I've admitted them to myself?

Murderer.

How am I going to explain to my family that I'm now engaged thanks to Cora?

Lock her up and throw away the key.

Peeling myself away from the wood, I finally turn to face the room. It's like stepping back in time, all of those historical romance films mum would play on the TV growing up had rooms just like this. The large four poster bed is fit for a king with its ornate carvings of cherubs and Gods. I note that there's nothing modern about this room, no telltale signs that we're even still in the 21st century.

I walk over to the arched crosshatched windows, it's still the dead of night but I'm sure I can see a pond out there in the distance. Turning to the other side where a smaller door stands, I walk over and open it to find the bathroom with, thankfully, modern appliances inside. The very large, copper bathtub in the centre takes up most of the space in the room. I don't hesitate as I turn the taps and start running a bath, the noise drowning out my thoughts. I close my eyes for a second, then stand up again and unzip my dress, letting it fall into a ball on the floor.

Grabbing a bottle of lavender bubble bath, I add a generous amount to the water, not giving two shits how much this ridiculously expensive thing costs. *He can suck my dick if he thinks I'm not keeping my promise to him.*

The water is almost overflowing by the time I step into it, my skin stings thanks to all the tiny cuts and bruises I now have.

Once I settle in, I hear the door to the bedroom open. Closing my eyes, I dunk my head beneath the water. When I come back up I gasp as I'm met with his gaze.

"I don't want to talk to you," I say as I begin scrubbing myself with a loofah.

"Fine," he mutters, glancing at the water and then heading back into the bedroom.

I scowl slightly as I hear shuffling from the next room. The next thing I know he's walking in completely naked, sending my pulse skyrocketing. I cover my eyes dramatically, "Can you please not wave that thing around?!" I shout as I feel the water rise as he steps into the tub. I guess I know now why it's extra large.

My blood boils as I think about how many women he's had in here. I remove my hand and narrow my eyes at him,

"So, what? We're sharing bath water now?" I snarl.

"Stop talking and turn around." My breath hitches at his commanding tone, but I do as he says as a tingle of excitement spreads through me. I keep my eyes on the silver curtains framing the small window, I hadn't noticed it before. My cheeks heat as I realise I should have definitely drawn the curtains before I got naked in a stranger's home. His hands start to massage my head gently and I realise he's washing my hair.

"What are you doing?" I ask softly as I lean into his head scratches.

"Your hair is thick with blood, it's going to take more than a quick dunk to get out."

I grin a little as he starts to make circles in my hairline.

"Why?" I say as I close my eyes.

"Because I can't take away what you did, I'm not like Zach, I can't take your memories or make them hazy. But I can help you wash it away."

I glance over my shoulder at him, he leans in and kisses my back gently.

"Tell me to stop," he says as he kisses me more and I feel myself moving towards him until his hard chest is flush to my back.

I rest my head back, feeling comforted by his skin. His fingers trace up my arm towards my shoulder and down towards my breast.

"Tell me to stop." His breath on my ear sends shivers down my spine as he travels further down my body. His touch is electric as he explores me. For a moment I'm utterly lost in him as he slides his fingers between my folds, his finger pressing hard against my clit and I revel in it. I slide my hand up behind him and grip the back of his neck while I widen my legs, allowing him full access to me.

His other hand wraps around my neck and squeezes,

"You like that, Garrick?"

I moan as his breath hits my ear again as the tension in my stomach builds, knowing his words will be undoing if I don't focus. I don't want this to end. I want to be trapped in this bathtub for the rest of my existence, drowning in pleasure and thinking of nothing else but him and all of the filthy things I want him to do to me.

"Words, please." He commands.

"Yes." I manage to say, my throat dry and hoarse from the screaming.

He pushes two fingers inside me and I lean back further into him, grabbing his neck harder as the pressure in my stomach increases. I ride his fingers, grinding as hard as I can as he hooks them around and caresses my insides, a move of his which I've come to appreciate. I clench around his fingers, finally reaching my climax. His fingers don't stop, he lets me ride out my pleasure before he stills. I slump back against him,

"I don't want it to end," I say breathlessly.

"It doesn't have to," he says as he nips my earlobe, turning me on again in an instant. "Just say the words, say you'll be mine."

I melt into his words, thinking only of having this feeling for the rest of my life. But now isn't the time to be thinking with my reproductive organs, there's a conversation to be had and I did vow to destroy his life. No matter how conflicted I am, I need to stay impartial, I can't make a decision based purely on the fact that this man is great in bed.

I pull away and turn towards him, the water splashing slightly with the motion. I wrap my legs around his waist and he pulls me in close, his eyes heating as I feel his hard cock against me. I gaze at him desperately as I rub myself against him.

"I have an eternity to give you the answers you crave," he says as his tongue darts out and licks my lips in one smooth movement.

I groan as he rubs himself harder on me, creating a friction I didn't know I needed right now.

"Let me be your distraction."

I take a sharp inhale at his words. A distraction. I can compartmentalise that.

I watch as he tilts his head back, letting out a gruff, "Fuck" as I impale myself on him slowly. His eyes snap back to mine, and it looks like what little self control he has left is about to snap as he sits up from the back of the tub and drives into me further in one hard thrust. But this is my time, *he* is here to fulfil *my* every desire. Benjamin Grenville does not get to be in control today.

"No," I say harshly as I slam my palms against his chest and shove him back with a thud. I lean in close to him as I reposition myself,

"You're not allowed to touch." The words tumble out of me and I watch a flicker of curiosity light up his eyes. He nods, a little warily and I begin my torture.

I fuck him slowly, intimately, determined to make this the best sex he's ever had. I slide up and down him, moaning loudly, not giving a fuck if Zach can hear me as I use him in everyway I possibly can. He bites his lip and his hands slide up my thighs and grip my waist. He doesn't try to adjust my speed, but I can see his inner turmoil each time I slide back down his dick.

He finally snaps and he hoists me up from the tub in one impressive movement. He climbs out and slams me against the wall, filling me further and making my eyes roll back into my head. I want to keep him, I've always wanted to keep him and I know in that moment as his cock hits that sweet spot that it doesn't matter what the truth is. At this moment it doesn't matter what he's done. We're just two people who want to drown in something good, even if it's just for a moment.

Chapter 31:

We lie there, naked and tangled up in the silver sheets, sweaty and panting for what feels like an eternity. Our limbs are entwined and my head lies heavily on his chest. His heartbeat is a comforting sound, I let it drown out every other thought that creeps back in. Neither of us want to move, the unspoken reason why hangs between us. We both know that the moment he speaks his truth, everything changes. Nothing will be as it was.

My stomach growls and I look up at him, slightly embarrassed by how loud it is.

"What do you need?" he asks sleepily.

I love him like this, relaxed and hazy. "Food," I say with a laugh, then a question comes tumbling out before I can stop it. "Do you... eat?" I look at him nervously, but he bursts into a howling fit of laughter.

"Of all the questions in the world you could ask, that's the one you pick first?" I slap his chest playfully, feigning annoyance.

"I think it's a valid question," I say as I plant a kiss on his chest, he groans and cups my chin bringing my lips up to his. He kisses me softly, and I melt into him. He groans again.

"You, will be the death of me," he says between kisses. I laugh against his lips,

"Benjamin Grenville defeated by a woman with a high sex drive."

He holds me close to his face, his hands gripping my damp hair.

"That's the first time you've ever called me Benjamin," he says, his eyes flicking down to my lips and he smirks.

"Are you getting soft on me, Louisa?"

He watches my reaction, I love hearing my name on his lips. Then again, I also don't mind when he calls me Garrick during a hate fuck. I raise an eyebrow at him,

"Are we on a first name basis now? This seems pretty serious." I laugh, basking in this perfectly human moment we were having.

"As much as I'd like this moment to last forever, I'm going to get you some food. Then once you've eaten, or while you eat if you like... I'll tell you my story."

Butterflies rise up in my stomach.

"I'll be back," he says as he kisses my forehead and gets out of bed.

Once he's out of the room, I get up and wander over to the suitcase sitting in the back corner of the room. I rifle through it and find a comfortable, black, cotton loungewear set. I throw it on and head back into the bathroom with my wash bag, giving my hair a brush and braiding it tight against my scalp. I let my mind occupy itself with the rhythm of it until I hear the door open and close and take a deep breath as I walk back in.

He's brought up a steaming hot bowl of beef stew, it smells incredible as he sets it down on the side table by the window and gestures for me to take a seat. I press my lips into a hard line as I head over, eager to hear it but I don't think it's going to change how I feel about him. The butterflies aren't there because I'm nervous or afraid, they're there because I can't wait to get to know him better. I *want* to know him better.

"You talk, I'll eat," I say as I sit down and he takes a seat at the edge of the bed, resting one leg on top of the other. Another casual gesture that I like. I pick up the spoon and dive in, never taking my eyes from his.

"It was the late 1500s that I was born. Unlike what you see now, my family wasn't always as wealthy. My father was a blacksmith who got lucky in a game of cards, he was always a very ambitious man that believed he was meant for better things. Not much has changed in the sense that opportunity only arises to those born into fortune.

He heard from a friend one night that there would be some friends of the Queen coming to visit our village, so, he put on his finest clothes and ventured into town and cheated a very wealthy Lord out of his title and lands. After that he sold our forge, and moved us into the Lord's manor, sparing no expense in the luxury we were not accustomed to.

The money was running low and fast, so my father decided to get lucky once more. High society never saw him coming, he cheated his way through half of England and each time a Lord thought he could beat him, or prove that his tricks were false- he took more than what they had.

Just five years after the first bit of luck, we were the richest family in England with all of the nobles sat tightly under our thumbs. While my father had all the power- it was quite a different experience for me and Zach. We were blacksmith boys, through and through. No matter how much money our father poured into our education, no matter how many times we strived to be better at disguising our heritage, it made no difference. High society saw right through us and shunned us all the same." I shifted awkwardly in my seat, the similarities in our stories was not something I had expected.

"Zach was a very protective older brother. Due to his heritage, he had become accustomed to the insults thrown at him throughout his life. But I wasn't, there were more times than I would like to admit that Zach had earned his name of being the loose cannon because of my insecurities. It's one of the reasons he attacked the Viscount at dinner after he insulted you. I can't put it into words but, I see so much of myself in you. On your first day when you were paraded around like a lamb to the slaughter... It brought up some things that I had long since buried." My heart pounds as my spoon shakes in my hand, it was all finally starting to click together. He sighs and runs a hand through his dishevelled hair, his eyes a million miles away. I focus on the stew and how the comforting heat warms my bones, not on the tears that threaten to fall from my eyes.

"Our father didn't help the situation, there were a lot of occasions where we were beaten to the brink of death because we slurped soup from a bowl instead of a spoon. The only reason he didn't actually kill us was because it would mean the death of his bloodline. All he ever cared about was his hard work continuing once he was gone from this world. I imagine him to be very proud at how far we've come. One night, my father told me that we're to pack our things and leave for court immediately, that we had marriages to secure and alliances to build. We did as we were told and played our roles of the devoted sons despite missing that forge so keenly.

Once we got to court, we realised very quickly that we were now entering a whole new playing field. The secrets and the drama were enough to keep you looking over your shoulder, but the murders? People did far worse for far less to obtain a position less sought after than my fathers and, let's just say, the school bullies were nothing compared to the king's advisors.

Every night there would be a banquet, celebrating the new king and the peace he had brought to our realm. But he was paranoid and egotistical, my father preyed on this. He told him fantastical stories of a golden chalice hidden in a place only he knew about, told to him apparently by some merchants who worked for him. The king lapped it up, his obsession driving him to appoint my father as Hand of the King, and that was my father's biggest mistake. Jealous rivalry alongside opposing faiths make a murderous bunch, they slaughtered my father in his bed the same night as the king announced it, leaving us to fend for ourselves, two orphaned pups amongst a hungry pack of wolves.

They feared us thanks to Zach and his extraordinary gift for torture, and I had lived in fear for so long that I had made it my business to always be one step ahead of them.

The king started to grow impatient, wanting us to reveal the location of the chalice that granted eternal life. Of course we knew it was all a lie, but the king made it very clear that we needed to deliver him our father's promise or we'd both be dead by the end of the year. We spent months researching, chasing every lead we could think of to save our necks and came up empty handed every single time. The king had declared that we were to leave for our mission within the week, his health was deteriorating rapidly and he grew more paranoid of a lurking usurper by the day. So I did the only thing I could think of to save my brother and me, I travelled back to our village where I met with the new owner of our forge.

He was dumbstruck when he saw me, I thought he looked familiar but I couldn't place his face. I questioned him to see if he knew of the merchants my father had dealt with previously. He sent me on a wild goose chase until I finally found him, except he wasn't a merchant at all. It was a woman that lived deep in the woods surrounded by moss and decay, I'll never forget the stench of her hovel as we entered. It was there that we discovered our father's greatest secret. His tricks were not tricks at all, he had sold his soul to her.

The woman practised magic, among other questionable things. I was dubious at first, until she told me things that only my father could have known. I fetched my brother at once and returned to her the same day. She performed a ritual on us in exchange for our own souls.

We were young and stupid and not accustomed to reading the fine prints of binding magical contracts. The ritual was... painful. It required us to surrender ourselves to the darkest of magic, the feel of it spreading through me was like suffocating in thick toxic smoke. I screamed and riled but never gave up. That determination to best the poncey lords at the king's side was too great, what more could a man in his twenties want than to be in control of his own destiny." He stops, rubbing his hands over his face, the memories clearly painful for him to relive.

Me, I'm frozen, lost in a time that I'd never known.

"When we woke, we were stronger and faster than before. We didn't need to eat or drink to survive. We don't need to do anything but exist. The price, of course, is heavy, to live without a soul is an empty feeling indeed, I'm incapable of feeling anything but anger and regret, yet I cannot be killed."

I'm on my feet instantly, gliding towards him, I take his head in my hands as I let my tears fall.

"I know that's not true, so do you." I graze his cheeks with my thumbs.

"I do, because when I met you I discovered that I can feel. I wasn't damned to a miserable life of torment afterall, even if that torment meant I had to follow around a foul-mouthed girl from Birmingham to do it." I snort as I wipe the tears away on my sleeve,

"What happened next? After you woke?" His lips pull up into a menacing smirk.

"We killed them all, Louisa," he says, tucking a stray lock of hair that has fallen from my messy bun behind my ear.

"We told the king that the chalice couldn't be moved, knowing that he would never even try to make the journey. The man was desperate, not stupid. England was still volatile at that point so to leave the throne unattended would have spelled disaster for us all. You read what happened next. We killed the leaders, left their sons and told them to swear fealty to us- most did. Those families are still around today, you met some of them at the dinner."

"Are they... the same people as before?" I ask tentatively.

"No, we can share our gift if we choose but only when they have something that we want in return. We've never given full immortality to anyone and we've never shared the secret on how it happens. So the ones at the dinner were only perhaps 70 to 80 years old. They won't live much longer though, I grow bored of their petty games. I always enjoy fresh blood on my council." I cringe a little, the question burning on my lips.

"No, we don't drink blood. We don't have fangs. We don't turn into bats." He smiles as he traces circles on my thighs.

"Your eyes, were they always silver?"

"No, they're the only part of me that ages. If you ever look into an elderly person's eyes, you'll see their colour has faded. Mine were once blue, Zach's were brown."

I furrow my brows as I try to recall various science lessons that might have explained that, but my head pounds from his revelations.

"Do you need some rest? We can continue tomorrow, I have all the time in the world."

I stop twiddling my thumbs and look up at him, the exhaustion finally hitting me.

"Do you sleep?" I ask, remembering a book I read as a teen where the vampire didn't sleep. I don't know how comfortable I'd be sleeping with him staring at me all night.

"Yes, I sleep," he chuckles and kisses my nose playfully, a devastatingly sweet side of him I'm yet to explore.

The action takes me aback, it's so at odds with his usual serious demeanour. "Tomorrow then, tell me more," I say, resting my forehead against his shoulder, sleep threatening to take me now that I've been fed.

"If I'm going to figure out what I'm going to do, I'll need more."

I move away from him and climb into the bed, when my head hits the pillow, peaceful darkness takes me instantly. I embrace it, like greeting an old friend.

Chapter 31:

I woke up the next day feeling rested, but the bed was empty. I don't remember falling asleep. Pulling the sheets up around me further, I inhale the scent of him like it will be the last time. I still don't know what I'm going to do, how a relationship with him could even work? Would it work? Did he even want a relationship with me? A ringing sound coming from the corner of the room pulls me from my tormented brain, I hurry out of the bed and pull out the burner phone my brother had given me all those months ago. The name flashing on the screen makes my stomach drop. Oscar.

I answer it and say nothing as I press it against my ear, trying to still my shaking hand.

"I see you've made yourself comfy with that cunt of a boyfriend. He's hard to get at you know, but I'll tell you who wasn't."

I frown at the sound of a muffled voice coming from down the line and my heart stops.

"Your dad had just stepped out of the gates when I took him. Poetic really, he only got to breathe once as a free man before I smacked him around the back of the head. He put up a good fight, he's still got it in him. But not quite the terrifying king I remember anymore."

He laughs sadistically as the muffled noise grows louder. There's a thud that makes me flinch, the noise stops. My breaths become shallow and raspy as I try to process the information.

"Your boyfriend didn't assign any of his mates to pick him up, so if you want someone to blame, blame him."

"I will destroy you, Oscar." My voice is a primal growl. My heart pounding in my ears. I need to think, but my brain is nothing more than a black cloud of fear.

"Don't be like that, you know all I want is to have you back home with me where you belong. I'll text you the address and I'll let your dad go as soon as you get here. And don't get any ideas, if you bring that boyfriend of yours I'll shoot your Dad. You know me, it's not an empty threat, it'll be like putting down an old dog."

"I understand," I say as I hang up. Pulling out my clothes from the bag, I don't waste time wallowing in my choices being taken away from me again by this man. He has me backed into a corner, I have no choice but to obey.

I get dressed and grab the burner, shoving it into my pocket alongside my wallet. If I'm to be on the run, I'll have to travel light. I pick up my normal phone and sob as I text Benjamin my pathetic excuse for a goodbye. I have to disappear, I can't have him looking for me. Not that I'm even sure that he would.

"I can't do this. I'm leaving. Don't look for me." I hit send and rush out of the room, not allowing myself to think about what I'm doing. If I think about it, I'll crumble. The thought of leaving Benjamin like this... after everything. I have to focus. My dad has spent the last four years in prison because of me, because of what I did. I owe him this. I owe him everything.

Making my way down to the entrance, I fling the door open as quietly as I can, the fresh air clearing my head instantly. I look for a car, I have no idea where I am but if I can just start driving I'm sure I can figure it out. Looking around I see two sports cars parked up in the driveway. I rush over to the black one, wondering if it'll be unlocked. I've hotwired plenty of cars during my rebellious teenage years, but never one like this. I yank the door open and my eyes fall on the keys still in the ignition.

"Wow, you really don't give a fuck, do you?" I almost laugh at my luck as I slide in and start the engine. I reverse out of the spot a little clumsily, it's been a long time since I've driven a manual. Sticking it in first, I glance in the mirror and my heart stops as I see a shirtless Zach Grenville standing on a balcony, sipping from a cup.

Don't look for me, it's better this way. I shout in my mind, not waiting for a response or stopping to wonder if he's even heard me, I dont know what this guys mind fuck range is. I speed off down the driveway, spinning the wheels as I try to drive as quickly as I can away to Oscar's meet point.

I'VE KEPT MY MIND OCCUPIED on the trip back to Birmingham, thankful I'd only been about three hours away. As I pull up in front of a sordid establishment I recognise as one we used to own. The garish neon lights that hang outside are off with it only being 11am, everyone this side of the cobbled streets are still asleep. The underworld of Birmingham only comes alive in the shadows. The street is silent as I get out of the car, my legs stiff from the journey and relishing in the sudden stretch. I pause before I enter. I've gone through every possible scenario on the way here. I had planned on entering this as a calm negotiator, but by the way the adrenaline is coursing through my veins, I think it's safe to say that won't be happening today.

As my hand touches the cold metal door, rage engulfs every other feeling. I yank it open and storm into the place, willing to put up a damn good fight if I need to. I am by no means a trained fighter, but I know that Oscar's men aren't either. I can probably pick them off one by one if I want to, Oscar's made it very clear that it's me he wants, so I doubt anyone will try to attack me. *Giving me the upper hand.*

I'm greeted with an eerie silence, as I step into the dark nightclub. There's nobody on the poles, no music, no bartenders. This reeks of a trap. Maybe I should've stopped to think about this. *Too late now*, I head for the door behind the stage that I'm guessing leads to the back room. My pulse beats hard against my neck.

I begin my walk down the shabby corridor, the smell of sweat and iron fills my senses as I gaze up at the flickering orange ceiling light.

"Honey, I'm home," I shout menacingly into the empty space, I pause and hear a shuffling sound from the room furthest from me. I pick up my pace, reaching the door in seconds. I shove it open with as much force as I can muster. The door bangs off the wall with the force I pour into it. My eyes locked onto the figure slumped against the back wall, his face covered with a sack and hands bound. My stomach hits the floor as I recognise my dad's signature gold chain hanging from his neck. I rush over and rip the bag from his head, he startles awake and I dont hide the sobs that escape me as I assess the damage to his face. Two swollen black eyes, a busted cheek and a broken nose. I pull the gag from his mouth and he sighs in relief, sagging forward onto me- resting his head on my shoulder. I take a moment to just hold him for a while.

"Princess, when are you going to learn?" he croaks and I laugh between sobs.

I pull him off me and wipe away the floods of tears falling down my cheeks.

"I'm sorry." He gazes at me like I'm the centre of the world and my heart breaks. I have put this man through so much.

"I'm going to get you out, can you walk?"

He shakes his head with what little energy he has. "Broken leg," he manages to say, wincing slightly.

"I can take your weight, come on, let's get out of here." I start to pull him up but the sound of footsteps approaching brings me to a halt.

"Finally, I thought I'd have to break his other leg to hurry you up."

A snarl escapes my lips. I turn to face Oscar, taking a protective stance in front of my Dad. I curl my hands into fists, if he's going to hurt him, he'll have to go through me first.

"Go on then boys, I'm a man of my word, let him go."

I watch the men enter from behind him, I back away towards my dad to shield him more.

"Look at you, finally embracing who you are. Protecting what's left of your family legacy, ha!" Oscar sneers, licking his lips as he approaches.

"Your family legacy is mine, Lou, you belong to me, you always have."

His hand caresses my cheek and I slap it away in disgust.

"You don't get to touch me," I shout.

"We're walking out of here together, if you so much as get in my way- I'll be sure to bury you in an unmarked grave where your pathetic name will die with you."

He punches me hard in the face and I stumble backwards, hitting my head against the wall next to my dad but I don't let it stop me. This is good, I'm getting under his skin. There's no way he's leaving here alive if I don't try to buy us some time, not when Oscar has this kind of opportunity at his fingertips.

I ignore the pain surrounding my eye socket as I stand back up, holding onto the wall for purchase. I laugh sadistically as I turn to face him again, his expression furious.

"You always did have a weak punch. What's the matter, Oscar? Not man enough for a Garrick?"

He charges at me but I'm too quick as I dodge out of his way, letting him slam into the wall. I go for his thugs first, using the element of surprise to my advantage. I kick the smallest one straight in the stomach, sending him flying. The big one comes at me from behind and yanks me up by the hair, I grab onto his arm, using it like a monkey bar in a park as I swing forwards. I plant my feet firmly onto the wall and then propel myself backwards with as much force as I can muster. The move sends him off kilter and he falls to the floor with a thud. I groan as my back collides with his knee, I don't give myself time to think as I roll away from him. I begin searching the room for some kind of weapon but come up empty. I have to grab Dad and get the fuck out of here, how can I do that with how injured he is? I glance at him quickly and see him try to stand but then my face is met by Oscar's elbow. My nose makes a sickly crunching sound, blood bursting from it instantly. My eyes go out of focus and start streaming with hot tears as I clutch at the wound with shaking hands- the blood dripping uncontrollably.

My dad yells something I don't quite hear and I watch him charge for Oscar, my heart breaking at his slowness. The once mighty lion who could bring a man to his knees with a simple roar, can barely stand straight. Oscar pushes him down to the floor and I run to him.

"No more games, Louisa."

The sound of my name on his lips makes my skin crawl.

"I will kill him, right here, right now if you don't stop this shit," he shouts as he pulls a gun from his pocket.

Looking back down at my dad, I put my hand against his face,

"I can't run anymore," I say between sobs.

"Oscar's going to take you to a hospital, I'll be fine here. He won't hurt me."

His eyes well up and he grabs my hand, squeezing it gently.

"I can't get us out of this one, princess," he says, kissing it roughly.

"I'll come back for you, as soon as I'm better. I'll burn this shithole to the ground for you, my darling."

I nod my head, knowing I'll probably never see him again. I'll be forced underground and kept at Oscar's side at all times like a caged bird.

"I'll see you soon." I lie.

I give him my best smile, my tears hitting his face like soft rain on a winter's day.

He's torn away from me then, leaving me empty and alone in this dingy room that resembles a prison cell. I keep my eyes to the floor, disassociation settling in, wrapping itself around me like an ironclad suit of armour, my father's empty promises all I have left. That and the memories of a silver eyed man plucked straight from a dark fairy tale.

Time seems to still as I sit there on the cold wooden floor, covered in my own blood. I wonder what will happen now. What he will do with me now that he has me?

I don't hear him come back into the room until he's inches from my face,

"Now, it's time for our forever," he says, smiling at me.

I look up into his eyes and feel bile rise up in my throat. I spit in his face, with as much force as I can muster, spraying him with blood and saliva. He grabs my neck roughly and pulls me closer to his face, the smell of him being this close was nauseating.

"You will respect me!" he shouts in my face as he fumbles with something in his pocket.

I hope it's a gun. But I know him better than that. Whatever fate he has in store for me won't involve a quick death. I feel a tiny prick in my neck and a hot liquid courses through my veins, my eyes widen as all that fear and rage I had felt is replaced with a euphoria unlike anything I've ever experienced. I tilt my head back to see the ceiling move and twirl into shapes I've never seen before. My eyes grow heavy and I give myself over to the calm.

"That's it, just relax."

I feel my body slump against something cold as my eyes finally close.

3 Months Later

Chapter 33:

Ben

I set down my journal on the table next to me, rougher than intended, I watch the China cup fall to the floor in slow motion and smash into a thousand tiny pieces. I can feel my control slipping further into the abyss. What little humanity I have left fades more with each day she is gone.

Today's journal entry is a detailed plan on how I might persuade the king to bring back being hung, drawn and quartered. That's just the beginning of what I want to do with the who thought it was a good idea to take what is *mine*. I muse over the simpler times. History proves that fear is the only way to rule and I've clearly lost my touch.

I stretch my legs as I stand and wander over to the wardrobe full of black suits. I stare at them aimlessly, wondering what the point of all this fuckery is. *Nothing matters without her.* My new mantra, in her absence.

I catch a glimpse of my reflection in the mirror hung on the wall next to me. I hardly recognise myself. It has been three long months since Louisa left and I found her father murdered on the side of the road- I've neglected myself since. Instead of taking care of myself and my business, I have poured every fucking resource at my disposal into finding where the little cunt has taken her. We tracked the car to the arse end of Birmingham, only to find it left burning outside a Strip Club. Not that I care. Material things no longer matter to me, without her everything is so fucking pointless.

I run my hand over my face, the stubble pricking my skin as Zach's voice fills my head,

If you're done feeling sorry for yourself, Frankie found her. She's back in Birmingham.

Excellent.

He's been moving her to a different spot in the country every few days, everytime we have a lead he always seems to be one step ahead. Frankie has been a blessing in disguise, working day and night to upturn all of his usual hiding spots. He'd been exceptionally gleeful when I gave him my personal mercenaries to help, the man is like a bloodhound. I've come to appreciate his blood thirst as well as his quick wit. I'll have to put him through proper training once all this is over.

"*Get your shit together, brother. Let's go get your girl.*"

I roll my eyes as I begin to shave the fur from my face, Zach has been my rock despite being half-crazed himself when she left. He thought she'd left of her own accord after I spilled our little secrets, but I knew something was wrong as I felt her emotions flood through the house that morning. I'd been careful with what I initially told her, I didn't want to reveal just how deep our heritage went.

Frankie's here, we're good to go.

I quicken my pace, letting a slither of my true power out to get the job done faster. When I am done getting ready to burn Birmingham to the ground, I head out of the hotel room and meet them in the restaurant.

Frankie, of course, is stuffing his face like the pig he'd been raised as while Zach leans against the bar, nursing a drink despite it being 7:30am.

You must have a clear head today, brother.

I'm cautious with my tone as I grab the pitcher of fresh orange juice sitting in the middle of the table and pour myself a glass. Zach glances over to me, his expression blank.

You're the one with clouded judgement, brother. All of this effort for some girl you've known for five minutes. Anyone would think you had a soul.

His sarcasm is out in full force today, which makes me nervous. They're not telling me something, I can practically taste the lie on my tongue.

"What's your intel?" I ask blankly to Frankie.

He stares up at me and cocks his head to the side.

"He's getting sloppy, he thinks he's outsmarted you. I heard from Alice, the prozzie I told you about. I told her to call me if she ever saw her, last night she did." He grins and leans back in his chair, pulling out a packet of cigarettes and lights one, handing it to me.

"Anyway, she sucked Oscar's newly promoted body guard's tiny little dick and he was more than happy to spill all of the cunt's secrets." He spits on the floor, a mannerism of his I've become accustomed to.

"There's more," I say, savouring the taste of the cigarette. I know what kind of man Oscar is, the nightmares of everything he could be doing to her have not been easy to tame- even with my big brother's gift.

Frankie clenches his jaw and sniffs before pulling out another cigarette, this time for himself. He takes a long drag and it damn near snaps what patience I have left.

Zach joins us finally at the table, giving Frankie a nod of approval and I find the interaction odd. He takes a deep breath much like mine before telling me where my fiancée is.

"She's being kept close to him, he doesn't let her out of his sight. She has a chain around her wrist apparently, one that he holds like a fucking leash. She's thin and he keeps her drugged up. Heroin the bloke told Alice. He said he's trying to make her so dependent on him that even if you do show up, she won't want to go."

My instincts heighten to a level I never knew I was capable of. My focus sharpens to the point where I can see where every speck of dust lays in this room. I hear Zach and Frankie's erratic heartbeats loudly in my ears as if I am pressed up against their chests. I close my eyes and clench my teeth together, fighting for what little control I have left.

Easy, brother.

Easy? Easy?! He's got her chained to him. He's giving her drugs to make her depend on him. Her life is ruined, Zach. I should have torn his head from his body when I had the chance, the moment I set eyes on him.

And now you can. We have the location and we're leaving now. We need her alive, it doesn't matter if she comes back broken, she just needs to live.

I meet his eyes the moment mine open, the silver twins of mine staring back at me. Zach has spent his entire life concerned for me, the unhinged, doting older brother who chose power over everything. The one who would do it again and again if it meant he could rule the world without limitations. I'm beginning to think he has the right idea. We'd gone soft, out of touch with the new digital age.

Fear is power, and it's time for the world to be reminded of that.